鬼書1

THE BOOK OF GHOSTS BOOK 1

敢不敢?! 看鬼故事學英文

子星 編著

Preface
序言

　　很榮幸有此靈感，在教學多年之後撰寫一本貢獻與激發有關語文方面，讓學習者對於學習英文能夠感到更有興趣與熱情的一本略爲「恐怖」卻有趣的書。從美國教書回來所獲得深刻的感觸是，無論是在美國學校的課堂上，或者在國內教育機構的課堂中，一位對語文教學充滿熱忱的老師，其最大的特色莫過於像一位神奇的魔法師，能將學習語文做全新的排列組合，並巧妙地轉變成一件讓學生感到快樂、有意義、有效果的學習活動。其中教學極大的重點就是：能激發起學生高度的學習動機。從此課堂上，不再是一個混亂或枯燥無味的學習環境。由此可見，老師教學方法的設計與教材內容的選用，對於瞭解其學生需求，與確實能提高學生學習興趣與動機，兩者實屬皆具同等重要性。身爲教育從業人員，需深知教育乃爲百年樹人之大計。期許有志於教育事業辛苦的老師與同業們，終能讓學習語文成爲是有成效、充滿樂趣，並能持之以恆的經驗，與編寫鬼書之目的如出一轍。

　　針對本書的特點，在此做主要的介紹。此書與一般市面上英文讀物最大的不同，除了書中驚悚性內容之外，此書主要是依據，並精挑細選教育部大考中心所公佈之7000單字，與非常重要且常見生活化升學考試用之片語，作為編寫本書故事之基礎。因此，經由研讀本書所學習到的重要內容之一，將幫助學習者掌握考試必備最為重點之單字與片語，並能有效地使用此書來準備參加各類型之英文考試。同時，從閱讀驚異的故事，也能進一步加深讀者英文的閱讀理解能力。總之，這是一本非常實用、有效果的英文讀本、輔助工具書。此外，針對此書設計與使用有四方面之要點，請參考如下精要之說明：

1. 此書故事呈現為文圖並茂，尤其搭配繪製彩色逼真的插圖，與書中採用中英文對照，重要單字、片語就隱藏在故事中有意義的方式編排，來幫助讀者有效率地學習。並且，7000單字中所選列重要的字彙，在中文故事中皆清楚標示出其相關Level 1～6程度難易符號。其中，未標示此符號者，則包括可能是少數較難、特殊，或可能因故事內容用字需求等，而無可避免未能涵蓋於7000單字中的字彙。因此，此書期能讓學習者深入內文情節的同時，也方便與加強學習者學習、記憶7000單字。此外，英文故事中所列舉之單字（與中文故事同）、片語，分別使用淡紅色標示為單字，淡藍色標示為片語，並依序以數字編號排列，作為讀者文後容易查詢相關解釋之用。英文故事中包含些許爲7000單字，卻未被選列於文後加以解釋者，則通常爲較簡單的用字，故而加以省略。

2. 文後每章重要單字與片語解釋的部分，也皆儘量標示出大考中心公佈7000單字中，所強調程度難易符號（含片語中所包含之7000單字）。換言之，全書明確標示出國中、小所必考之1000、1200、2000單字，與升大學7000單字中，Level 1～6的程度難易符號，期望與鼓勵讀者能以循序漸進的方式熟悉、學習與記憶重要的英文單字、片語。也就是，幫助讀者學習英文，基本上先對於單字程度作通盤的認識與瞭解，進而奠定良好單字、片語使用，和長久記憶的方向與基礎。此外，依照學習者不同個別的需求與使用此書的情況，亦能有效使用此書準備多項重要相關語言考試，如：英文科升學考試、全民英檢、多益、托福、通用英檢等考試。

3. 文後單字與片語解釋中，儘量列舉單字多項最重要或最常用的中文解釋（包括單字不同詞性有不同的意思解釋），及其延伸片語的使用。並更進一步選列更多其它與7000單字相關字彙與重要片語之使用，再加上常見重要之諺語。完整加強、豐富與提升學習者學習準備重要單字、片語的能力。又文後故事單字有多重意思解釋處，特別也作出明顯畫底線、顏色差異標示，以方便學習者辨識、明白單字於所屬故事文脈中清楚的意義，而避免產生混淆的現象。

4. 最後，隨書免費附贈英文故事MP3光碟作為發音示範，鼓勵讀者學習語言，切記能多聽、多練習，使能達成意想不到事半功倍的學習與記憶效果。

　　學習語言能學得好，有進步，最大訣竅在於有濃厚的學習興趣，加上如有效率的方法與工具書始能努力不懈。殷切期盼《鬼書 1 The Book of Ghosts Book 1》能提升學習英文興趣，讓讀者有絕佳的收穫，學習英文與參與各項考試都能大大地加分，並且語言能力更上一層樓。此書為個人利用繁忙課後之餘完成之作，難免有滄海遺珠之憾，還請不吝特惠指教，感謝！

作者 子星 謹識
2011　2月

Contents
目録

～ 第一章 ～

加拿大維修工人

這可能是個真實的（¹true）故事。大約三十年前，故事發生在加拿大（Canada），曾經被一份有名的（²famous）報紙報導（¹report）過。兩名受指派的（appointed）維修（⁵maintenance）工人，傑克和路克，接到一項任務（³mission），被加拿大政府（²government）派遣至非常遙遠的北方（²northern）地區（³territory）。它是一個靠近北冰洋的極地（⁵polar）邊境（⁵frontier）之處。這兩人必須在那裡修理（²fix）一個嚴重的（²serious）停電（blackout）問題（¹problem）。那裡的天氣是很善變的（³changeable）。雪（¹snow）正猛烈地（heavily）下著，所以在他們電力（³electrical）維修工作過程（³process）的期間，二位維修工人被迫找尋躲藏（²hide）進去鄰近的（neighboring）一間小

~ Chapter 1 ~
The Canadian
Maintenance Workers

This is possibly a [1]true story. It [2]took place in [3]Canada and was once [4]reported in a [5]famous newspaper about thirty years ago. Two [6]appointed [7]maintenance workers, Jack and Luke, got a [8]mission and were [9]sent by the Canadian [10]government to the far away [11]northern [12]territory. It was also a place near the [13]polar [14]frontier of the [15]Arctic Ocean. The two men had to [16]fix a [17]serious [18]blackout [19]problem there. The weather was very [20]changeable there. The [21]snow was falling [22]heavily, so in the [23]process of their [24]electrical maintenance work, the two maintenance workers were [25]forced to find and [26]hide in a [27]neighboring small [28]log cabin. The small log cabin had been [29]abandoned by [30]unknown [31]inhabitants [32]in the past long ago.

木屋中。小木屋在很久以前就被過往、未知的（unknown）居民（⁶inhabitant）所遺棄（⁴abandon）。他們希望能夠躲避過這一場凜冽（⁴severe）冬天中可怕的（²terrible）暴風雪（snowstorm）。

　　不幸地（unfortunately），過了不久之後（³afterwards），兩名之中的其中一名維修工人，路克，由於重感冒始生肺炎（pneumonia）而死（¹die）去。悲哀地，可憐的（¹poor）傑克被留下來獨自（¹alone）待（¹stay）在小木屋裡。他衷心期盼著這場大風雪（⁵blizzard）可能會很快地停止（¹stop）。傑克真的非常地（³badly）思念他的家人。他努力地（¹hard）試著計算（¹count）日子，以便能得知自從離開在溫哥華（Vancouver）的家有多久了。他臆測（¹guess）著很有可能地（probably）直到那個時候，他待在那裡已經有好幾個禮拜時間了。但是，在更細心地（closely）計算後，他開始抱怨（²complain）起來。事實上（actually），從離開他的家鄉（³hometown）溫哥華，來到這

They hoped they could ³³escape from the ³⁴terrible ³⁵snowstorm in the ³⁶severe winter.

³⁷Unfortunately, one of the two maintenance workers, Luke, ³⁸died not very long ³⁹afterwards, ⁴⁰due to ⁴¹pneumonia which had ⁴²set in from ⁴³a bad cold. Sadly, ⁴⁴poor Jack was ⁴⁵left behind to ⁴⁶stay ⁴⁷alone at the log cabin. He ⁴⁸looked forward to the great ⁴⁹blizzard possibly ⁵⁰stopping soon. Jack really missed his family ⁵¹badly. He tried ⁵²hard to ⁵³count the days ⁵⁴so that he could ⁵⁵get a clear picture of how long it had been since he left his home in ⁵⁶Vancouver. He ⁵⁷guessed that ⁵⁸probably up until then, he had been there for ⁵⁹a couple of weeks. But after counting more ⁶⁰closely, he started to ⁶¹complain. ⁶²Actually, it had been almost one month's time since he left his ⁶³hometown

麼貧瘠（⁵barren）、遙遠（²distant）、荒蕪（deserted）之地，
幾乎是快要一個月的時間了。那感覺如同置身於一個鳥不生蛋
的偏僻處。他必須像是一種慣例（³routine）來從事這樣沉重的
維修工作。而被雪困住在那兒，使他的心充滿著憤怒（¹anger）
與焦慮（⁴anxiety）。

在一天清晨，傑克聽到（¹sound）了什麼，聽起來像有
人正敲（²knock）著門的聲音。他起床走進舒適（⁵cozy）小木
屋中的飯廳。他深深地（deeply）感到震驚的（²shocked），
發現到在那大飯桌旁邊（⁶alongside），路克正坐在木製的
（²wooden）椅子的其中一張上。傑克甚至沒有為他開門呀！傑
克內心（mentally）害怕死了，心想著：「他不是已經死了嗎？
我不是幾天前把他的屍體埋（³bury）了嗎？為何他現在這裡
呢？」接著，身材圓胖的（⁵chubby）傑克，抓住（³grab）路克
僵硬的（⁵rigid）屍體，再次將他往小屋（⁴cottage）屋外埋了。
但似乎這種怪異的（⁵weird）情況（³situation）將從不會結束一

Vancouver to ⁶⁴come to this ⁶⁵barren, ⁶⁶distant, and ⁶⁷deserted place. It ⁶⁸felt like he was ⁶⁹in the middle of nowhere. He had to do this heavy maintenance work as ⁷⁰a sort of ⁷¹routine. Also, being ⁷²snowed in there made him ⁷³full of ⁷⁴anger and ⁷⁵anxiety.

On one early morning, Jack heard what ⁷⁶sounded like someone ⁷⁷knocking at the door. He ⁷⁸got up and ⁷⁹walked into the ⁸⁰dining room of the ⁸¹cozy log cabin. He was ⁸²deeply ⁸³shocked to find that Luke was sitting on one of the ⁸⁴wooden chairs ⁸⁵alongside the large dining table. Jack did not even open the door for him. Jack was ⁸⁶mentally ⁸⁷scared stiff to think, "Didn't he die already? Did I not ⁸⁸bury his body several days ago? Why is he here now?" Then, ⁸⁹chubby Jack ⁹⁰grabbed Luke's ⁹¹rigid body and buried him ⁹²once again outside the ⁹³cottage. But it seemed that this kind of ⁹⁴weird ⁹⁵situation would

樣。傑克於是意識到這樣的地方增加（¹grow）著一種可怕的（²fearful）氣氛（⁴atmosphere）。事情每況愈下，而且，這種情形持續超過了一個禮拜的時間。例如：每當（²whenever）在早上他聽見了有人敲門，傑克便知道路克又一次次地回來了。他又必須每次緊抓著路克的屍體，用盡全力將屍體往小屋外愈埋愈深，以便他可能擺脫之後（⁶thereafter）屢次的（³frequent）、繼續的（⁴continuous）一再出現（reappearance）路克的鬼魂（¹ghost）。

在另一天早上，他一醒來，傑克就又聽見了什麼，有如敲門的聲音。他再度地受到驚嚇的（startled）而很大聲地（loudly）尖叫（³scream）起來。因為他從未預期（⁶anticipate）死了的路克，將會重新出現在飯桌前。傑克馬上在恐慌（³panic）中大叫，而且嚇得發抖。他說著：「這實在是太可怕（³scary）、太無法理解（incomprehensible）了啊！為什麼正在

never [96]come to an end. Jack was then [97]conscious of a [98]fearful [99]atmosphere [100]growing in this place. Things [101]went from bad to worse, and it [102]lasted for over one week. [103]For example, [104]whenever he heard someone knock at the door in the morning, Jack knew Luke had [105]come back [106]again and again. He also had to grab Luke's body and [107]do his best in burying the body deeper and deeper outside the cottage [108]each time so that he could [109]get rid of the more [110]frequent and [111]continuous [112]reappearances of Luke's [113]ghost [114]thereafter.

On another morning, [115]as soon as he [116]woke up, Jack also heard what sounded like a knock at the door. He felt [117]startled again and [118]screamed very [119]loudly because he never [120]anticipated that dead Luke would reappear [121]in front of the dining table. [122]Right away, Jack [123]cried out in a [124]panic and [125]shivered with fear. "This is too [126]scary, too

發生（¹happen）這件事情呢？」因屈服於他內心的恐懼，傑克幾乎是快精神崩潰了。他然後使用了僅有的一把槍，一支來福槍（⁵rifle），而瘋狂地（crazily）對路克開槍（²shoot）了有幾秒鐘的時間。接著，傑克變得如此地歇斯底里（⁶hysterical），以至於他將路克的身體分屍了，並將它們埋在屋外不同的（¹different）地方。他做完這可怕的事情後，傑克感到很滿意的（satisfied），而在日記（²diary）其中的一頁（¹page）上寫下了一些字：「哈！哈！哈！路克，你完蛋了（finished）吧！你將再也永遠不會回來了吧！」於是，他毫無憂慮（¹worry）上床睡覺去了。可是，半夜時，突然地（suddenly）在他的夢中，傑克清楚地聽見了一些很大聲的敲門聲響，而害怕了大叫著：「路克！原諒（²forgive）我吧！」最後（finally），傑克射向他自己的頭部自殺了。

[127]incomprehensible! Why is this [128]happening?" he said. Because he [129]succumbed to the fear inside his heart, Jack almost had a [130]nervous breakdown. He then used the only gun he had — a [131]rifle, and [132]crazily [133]shot Luke [134]for seconds. Next, Jack became so [135]hysterical that he [136]cut Luke's body into pieces and buried them in [137]different places outside the cottage. After he did this terrible thing, Jack felt very [138]satisfied and [139]wrote down on one of the [140]pages of his [141]diary, "Ha! Ha! Ha! You are [142]finished! You will never ever come back again, Luke!" So, he [143]went to bed without a [144]worry. But, [145]at midnight, [146]suddenly, in his dream, Jack clearly heard some very loud knocking noises at the door and frightened, shouted, "[147]Forgive me, Luke!" [148]Finally, Jack [149]committed suicide by shooting himself in the head.

　　過了幾分鐘，小木屋的門被打開了。正站在門口那裡的竟是幾名救援（⁴rescue）人員，並不是路克的鬼魂！在他們聽到傑克射擊（gunshot）的槍聲之後，屋內傑克與路克的屍體就被救難人員發現（¹discover）了。根據專家（²expert）們的推測（⁶assumption），他們認為（²consider）路克是因為罹患某種疾病（illness）死亡的，而不是槍殺。而且，他的死亡時間是比起傑克死的時候更早得許多。此外（⁴furthermore），傑克死亡主要的（²main）原因（¹cause）可說完全（absolutely）是因為自殺。

　　可是，專家們指出傑克在自己的日記中奇怪地（strangely）提起（³mention）過，路克的屍體，在他死後仍然永不停止地（endlessly）再三出現。它只是傑克處於雪地之中遭受（²experience）發瘋（madness）的幻覺（⁶illusion）嗎？或著可能（¹possible）什麼一些心理學家（⁴psychologist）所說的話是正確的嗎？他們說道：「出自於他自己本身的寂寞

After ^{150}a few minutes, the door of the small log cabin was opened. Some ^{151}rescue workers were actually standing there at the door, not Luke's ghost! Jack's and Luke's bodies inside were ^{152}discovered by the rescue workers after they heard the sound of Jack's ^{153}gunshot. ^{154}According to ^{155}experts' ^{156}assumptions, they ^{157}considered that Luke was dead ^{158}because of an ^{159}illness and not a shooting. And the time of his death was much earlier than that of Jack's. ^{160}Furthermore, the ^{161}main ^{162}cause of Jack's death was ^{163}absolutely suicide.

But the experts ^{164}pointed out that Jack had ^{165}strangely ^{166}mentioned in his own diary that Luke's body kept ^{167}showing up again and again ^{168}endlessly after his death. Was it only Jack's ^{169}illusion while ^{170}experiencing ^{171}madness in the snow? Or was it ^{172}possible that what some ^{173}psychologists said was right? They said that ^{174}out of his own ^{175}loneliness, Jack ^{176}sleepwalked （loneliness），傑克晚上夢遊（sleepwalk）了。而且，他挖掘起路克的屍體，並將其屍體搬運（[1]move）回去木屋內；卻不知道他自己如此怪異的（[6]bizarre）行為（[4]behavior）。」

at night. He also [177]dug up Luke's body and [178]moved the body back to the log cabin without being [179]aware of his own [180]bizarre [181]behavior.

Chapter 1

Vocabulary

1. ¹true ［tru］（adj.）①眞的；確實的 ②忠誠的；忠實的
（phr.）①come true 實現 ②true to life（書、電影等）眞
實的；逼眞的 ③your true colors 本性；本來面目
【諺】Trust men and they will be true to you.
信人者人恆信之。
²trust（v.）信任
【相關字彙與重要片語】
²truth ［truθ］（n.）眞理；眞實；眞相 （phr.）to tell the
truth 說實話

2. ¹take ¹place（phr.）發生

3. Canada ［ˈkænədə］加拿大

4. ¹report ［rɪˈport］（v.）/（n.）報告；報導 （phr.）①report
card 成績單 ②of bad/good report 名聲壞/好
【相關字彙】
²reporter ［rɪˈportɚ］（n.）記者

5. ²famous ［ˈfeməs］（adj.）有名的；著名的 （phr.）be famous
for 以……有名
【相關字彙與重要片語】
⁴fame ［fem］（n.）聲譽；名望；名聲 （phr.）Walk of Fame

（好萊塢）星光大道

6. appointed [əˋpɔɪntɪd]（adj.）任命的；指派的
    【相關字彙與重要片語】
    ⁴appoint [əˋpɔɪnt]（v.）①任命；指派 ②指定（時間或地
    點）
    ⁴appointment [əˋpɔɪntmənt]（n.）①（正式的）約會；預約
    ②任命 ③職位 （phr.）make an appointment with Sb. 與某
    人定下約會

7. ⁵maintenance [ˋmentənəns]（n.）①維修 ②保持；主張 ③贍
    養費；生活費
    【相關字彙】
    ²maintain [menˋten]（v.）①維持；保持 ②堅持；主張 ③維
    修

8. ³mission [ˋmɪʃən]（n.）任務；使命
    【相關字彙】
    ⁶missionary [ˋmɪʃənˌɛrɪ]（n.）傳教士

9. ¹be ¹sent ¹to（phr.）被派到
    【相關字彙】
    ¹send [sɛnd]（v.）①寄；發送 ②派遣

10. ²government [ˋgʌvɚnmənt]（n.）①（常大寫）政府 ②政體；
    統治
    【相關字彙】
    ²govern [ˋgʌvɚn]（v.）①管理；統治 ②支配；控制

11. ²northern [ˋnɔrðən]（adj.）北部的；北方的 （phr.）northern hemisphere 北半球 ☆ ⁶hemisphere（n.）半球

【相關字彙】

¹north [nɔrθ]（n.）/（adj.）/（adv.）北方（的；地）；北部（的；地）

12. ³territory [ˋtɛrə͵torɪ]（n.）①領土；國土 ②<u>區域</u> ③（知識等）領域 （phr.）disputed territory 有爭議的領土

☆ ⁴dispute（v.）爭論

13. ⁵polar [ˋpolə]（adj.）①北極的；南極的；<u>極地的</u> ②極性的；電極的 ③正好相反的；截然對立的 （phr.）polar bear 北極熊

14. ⁵frontier [frʌnˋtɪr]（n.）國境；邊境

15. ⁶Arctic ¹Ocean（phr.）北冰洋

【相關字彙】

⁶arctic [ˋɑrktɪk]（n.）/（adj.）北極（的）

16. ²fix [fɪks]（v.）①使固定；安裝 ②<u>修理</u> ③確定；決定 （phr.）fix up ①修理 ②為……做安排 ③湊對；撮合（人）

17. ²serious [ˋsɪrɪəs]（adj.）①認眞的；嚴肅的 ②<u>嚴重的</u> （phr.）take St. seriously 對某事認眞

18. blackout [ˋblæk͵aʊt]（n.）停電

19. ¹problem [ˋprɑbləm]（n.）問題 （phr.）①no problem 沒問題；不客氣 ②sleep on a problem 把問題留到第二天解決

☆ sleep on St.（phr.）把某事留待第二天決定

20. ³changeable [ˋtʃendʒəbl̩]（adj.）易變的；善變的

21. ¹snow [sno]（n.）/（v.）雪；下雪　（phr.）snow-capped 積雪蓋頂的

    【相關字彙】

    ²snowy [ˋsnoɪ]（adj.）下雪的

22. heavily [ˋhɛvɪlɪ]（adv.）①沉重地 ②猛烈地

    【相關字彙與重要片語】

    ¹heavy [ˋhɛvɪ]（adj.）①沉重的 ②大量的；多的　（phr.）a heavy heart 心情沉重

23. ³process [ˋprɑsɛs]（n.）①過程 ②步驟；方法　（v.）①加工 ②處理

    【相關字彙】

    ⁵procession [prəˋsɛʃən]（n.）行列；行進

24. ³electric/³electrical [ɪˋlɛktrɪk]/[ɪˋlɛktrɪkl̩]（adj.）電的

    【相關字彙】

    ³electricity [ɪˏlɛkˋtrɪsətɪ]（n.）電；電力

25. ¹be ¹forced ¹to（phr.）被迫

    【相關字彙與重要片語】

    ¹force [fors]（n.）①力；力量 ②暴力；武力 ③有影響的人（或事物）　（v.）①強逼；迫使 ②勉強作（發）出　（phr.）①come into force（法律）開始生效 ②Air Force One 空軍一號（美國總統專用座機）

26. ²hide [haɪd]（v.）遮蔽；躲藏

【相關字彙】

hideout [ˈhaɪdˌaʊt] （n.）躲藏處

27．neighboring [ˈnebərɪŋ] （adj.）鄰近的

【相關字彙】

²neighbor [ˈnebɚ] （n.）鄰居

【諺】Love your <u>neighbor</u>, yet pull not down your fence.

害人之心不可有，防人之心不可無。

²fence （n.）籬笆　¹pull ¹down （phr.）拆毀

28．²log ³cabin （phr.）小木屋

【相關字彙與重要片語】

²log [lɔg] （n.）圓木　（v.）登入電腦系統　（phr.）log in 登入；　進入（系統）

³cabin [ˈkæbɪn] （n.）①小屋　②（飛機或船的）客艙

29．⁴abandon [əˈbændən] （v.）捨棄；拋棄　（phr.）abandon oneself to 沉溺於

30．unknown [ʌnˈnon] （adj.）未知的

31．⁶inhabitant [ɪnˈhæbətənt] （n.）居民

【相關字彙】

⁶inhabit [ɪnˈhæbɪt] （v.）居住；棲息於

32．¹in ¹the ¹past （phr.）在過去

33．³escape ¹from （phr.）躲避

【相關字彙】

³escape [əˈskep] （v.）①逃走；逃脫　②避開　（n.）逃亡；

逃開

34. ²terrible [ˈtɛrəb!] （adj.）①恐怖的；可怕的 ②極度的

35. snowstorm [ˈsnoˌstɔrm] （n.）暴風雪

【相關字彙】

²storm [stɔrm] （n.）暴風雨；風暴

36. ⁴severe [səˈvɪr] （adj.）①嚴重的；凜冽的 ②嚴厲的；苛刻的

37. unfortunately [ʌnˈfɔrtʃənɪtlɪ] （adv.）不幸地

【相關字彙與重要片語】

³fortune [ˈfɔrtʃən] （n.）①命運 ②財富 ③運氣 （phr.）①fortune teller 算命師 ②have one's fortune told 讓人算命；去算命 ③make a fortune 發財

⁴fortunate [ˈfɔrtʃənɪt] （adj.）幸運的；吉利的

38. ¹die [daɪ] （v.）死亡 （phr.）die in your bed 壽終正寢

【相關字彙與重要片語】

¹dead [dɛd] （adj.）死的；枯的

¹death [dɛθ] （n.）死；死亡 （phr.）life-and-death 生死攸關的

39. ³afterward/³afterwards [ˈæftəwəd]/[ˈæftəwədz] （adv.）之後；以後

40. ³due ¹to （phr.）由於

【相關字彙與重要片語】

³due [dju] （adj.）①應支付的 ②到期的 ③因為；由於

（phr.）in due course 在適當的時機

41. pneumonia [njuˋmonjə]（n.）肺炎

42. ¹set ¹in（phr.）（指雨、壞天氣、傳染等）開始並可能繼續下去

    【相關字彙】

    ¹set [sɛt]（v.）①放；置；豎立 ②使開始；使著手做 ③使處於（特定狀態）（n.）一部；一套；一副

43. ¹a ¹bad ¹cold（phr.）重感冒

44. ¹poor [pʊr]（adj.）①貧窮的 ②可憐的；不幸的

45. ¹leave ¹behind（phr.）留下

    【相關字彙與重要片語】

    ¹leave [liv]（v.）離開；出發；前往 （phr.）leave for 離去；動身

46. ¹stay [ste]（v.）①停留；待 ②保持 （n.）停留；逗留 （phr.）stay up 熬夜

47. ¹alone [əˋlon]（adj.）/（adv.）單獨的（地）

48. ¹look ²forward ¹to（phr.）期待

49. ⁵blizzard [ˋblɪzəd]（n.）暴風雪

50. ¹stop [stɑp]（v.）①停止 ②妨礙；阻止 （n.）①停止 ②停車站

51. ³badly [ˋbædlɪ]（adv.）①壞地 ②嚴重地 ③（口）極；非常地

52. ¹hard [hɑrd]（adj.）①堅硬的 ②艱難的 ③勤奮的 （adv.）

努力地;拼命地 (phr.) be hard on Sb. 嚴厲對待某人

53. ¹count [kaʊnt] (v.) ①數;計算 ②把……算在內 (phr.)
①count down 倒數計時 ②count in 把……算入
【相關字彙】
³countable [ˋkaʊntəbl̩] (adj.) 可數的
⁴counter [ˋkaʊntɚ] (n.) 櫃檯

54. ¹so ¹that (phr.) 如此……以至於

55. ¹get ¹a ¹clear ¹picture ¹of (phr.) 清楚了解
【相關字彙與重要片語】
¹clear [klɪr] (adj.) ①晴朗的;明亮的 ②清楚的 ③明顯的
(v.) 使乾淨;變清楚 (phr.) ①get clear out 水落石出
②in the clear 無危險的;償清債務的 ③clear the table 收拾
飯桌
⁶clearance [klɪrəns] (n.) ①清除 ②出清
¹picture [ˋpɪktʃɚ] (n.) ①圖畫 ②照片 ③想像;描寫
⁶picturesque [ˌpɪktʃəˋrɛst] (adj.) 圖畫般的

56. Vancouver [vænˋkuvɚ] (n.) 溫哥華

57. ¹guess [gɛs] (v.) / (n.) 推測;猜想 (phr.) anybody's
guess 誰也拿不準的事

58. probably [ˋprɑbəblɪ] (adv.) 大概地;很可能地
【相關字彙】
³probable [ˋprɑbəbl̩] (adj.) 大概的;很可能發生的

59. ¹a ²couple ¹of (phr.) 幾個;兩三個

【相關字彙】

²couple [ˋkʌpḷ]（n.）①一對；一雙 ②夫婦

60. closely [ˋkloslɪ]（adv.）接近地；細心地

【相關字彙與重要片語】

¹close [kloz]（v.）①關閉 ②（商店等）打烊；關門 ③結束

（n.）結束 （phr.）bring st. to a close 結束
某事

☆ ¹bring（v.）帶來；導致

＊[klos]（adj.）①接近的 ②（關係）親密的；緊密的
③周密的；精確的

61. ²complain [kəmˋplen]（v.）①抱怨 ②控訴 （phr.）complain
of/about 抱怨

【相關字彙】

³complaint [kəmˋplent]（n.）①抱怨 ②控訴

62. actually [ˋæktʃʊəlɪ]（adv.）①事實上地；真實地 ②竟然

【相關字彙】

³actual [ˋæktʃʊəl]（adj.）實際的；真實的

63. ³hometown [ˋhomˋtaʊn]（n.）故鄉；家鄉

64. ¹come ¹to（phr.）來到

65. ⁵barren [ˋbærən]（adj.）①貧瘠的；荒蕪的 ②（人）不生育
的 ③（植物）不結果實的

66. ²distant [ˋdɪstənt]（adj.）①遙遠的 ②疏遠的；冷淡的

【相關字彙與重要片語】

²distance [`dɪstəns]（n.）①距離 ②疏遠；冷淡 （phr.）
①in the distance 在遠處 ②keep Sb. at a distance 對某人不
友善；保持距離

67. deserted [dɪ`zɝtɪd]（adj.）荒蕪的；被遺棄的；無人住的
【相關字彙】
²desert [`dɛzət]（n.）①沙漠 ②賞罰（常用複數）
＊ [dɪ`zɝt]（v.）遺棄；拋棄

68. ¹feel ¹like（phr.）想要；感到好似

69. ¹in ¹the ¹middle ¹of ⁵nowhere（phr.）鳥不生蛋
【相關字彙】
⁵nowhere [`no͵hwɛr]（n.）無處；無地

70. ¹a ²sort ¹of（phr.）一種
【相關字彙】
²sort [sɔrt]（n.）種類
【諺】It takes all <u>sorts</u> to make a world. 一樣米養百種人。

71. ³routine [ru`tin]（n.）例行公事；日常工作

72. ¹be ¹snowed ¹in（phr.）被雪困住

73. (¹be) ¹full ¹of（phr.）充滿著
【相關字彙與重要片語】
¹full [fʊl]（adj.）①滿的；充滿的 ②吃飽的 ③完全的
（phr.）①full moon 滿月 ②have one's hands full 非常忙碌

74. ¹anger [`æŋgə]（n.）怒；生氣

75. ⁴anxiety [æŋ`zaɪətɪ]（n.）①焦慮；擔憂 ②渴望

76. ¹sound ［saʊnd］（v.）聽起來 （adj.）健全的；健康的
    （phr.）as sound as a bell 十分健康
    ☆ ¹bell（n.）鐘；鈴
    【諺】Empty vessels make the most sound. 空桶響叮咚。
    　　　³empty（adj.）空的　⁴vessel（n.）容器

77. ²knock ［nɑk］（v.）①敲；擊；打 ②相撞 （n.）敲門（聲）
    （phr.）knock off 停止；歇工

78. ¹get ¹up（phr.）起床

79. ¹walk ¹into（phr.）走進

80. dining ¹room（phr.）飯廳
    【相關字彙】
    ³dine ［daɪn］（v.）進食；用餐
    dining ［`daɪnɪŋ］（n.）進餐

81. ⁵cozy ［`kozɪ］（adj.）溫暖而舒適的；愜意的

82. deeply ［`diplɪ］（adv.）深地
    【相關字彙與重要片語】
    ¹deep ［dip］（adj.）深的 （phr.）in deep water（s）處於困
    境
    【諺】Still waters run deep. 大智若愚。

83. shocked ［ʃɑkt］（adj.）震驚的
    【相關字彙】
    ²shock ［ʃɑk］（n.）①撞擊；震動 ②震驚 （v.）使震驚

84. ²wooden ［`wʊdn̩］（adj.）木製的

【相關字彙】

^{1}wood [wʊd]（n.）①木材；木頭（單數）②樹林（複數）

85. ^{6}alongside [ə`lɔŋ`saɪd]（adv.）/（prep.）①在……旁邊 ②沿著……的邊 ③與……並排靠攏著

86. mentally [`mɛntḷɪ]（adv.）①內心地 ②精神上地 ③智力地

【相關字彙】

^{3}mental [`mɛntḷ]（adj.）①內心的 ②精神的 ③智力的

87. ^{1}be scared ^{3}stiff（phr.）非常害怕

【相關字彙】

^{1}scare [skɛr]（v.）/（n.）驚嚇；恐懼

scared [skɛrd]（adj.）吃驚的；恐懼的

^{3}stiff [stɪf]（adj.）①硬的；僵硬的 ②不自然的

88. ^{3}bury [`bɛrɪ]（v.）埋葬 （phr.）bury one's head in the sand 逃避現實

【相關字彙】

^{5}burial [`bɛrɪəl]（n.）埋葬；葬禮

89. ^{5}chubby [`tʃʌbɪ]（adj.）圓胖的；豐滿的

90. ^{3}grab [græb]（v.）抓取；搶奪 （phr.）grab at 奪得

91. ^{5}rigid [`rɪdʒɪd]（adj.）①僵硬的 ②嚴格的

92. ^{1}once ^{1}again（phr.）再一次

93. ^{4}cottage [`kɑtɪdʒ]（n.）①小屋 ②農舍

94. ^{5}weird [wɪrd]（adj.）怪誕的；神祕的；鬼怪似的

95. ^{3}situation [ˏsɪtʃʊ`eʃən]（n.）①情況 ②處境；境遇

96．¹come ¹to ¹an ¹end（phr.）結束

【相關字彙與重要片語】

¹end［ɛnd］（n.）①結局；死亡 ②末端 ③目的 （v.）①結束 ②死亡 （phr.）①end up with 以……結束 ②make ends meet 勉強維持生計；量入為出

【諺】All's well that <u>ends</u> well.

結果為好，一切都好。

【諺】You cannot burn the candle at both <u>ends</u>.

蠟燭勿為兩頭燒。

97．¹be ³conscious ¹of（phr.）意識到

【相關字彙】

³conscious［ˈkɑnʃəs］（adj.）①意識出；察覺出 ②有知覺的 ③故意的

98．²fearful［ˈfɪrfəl］（adj.）可怕的

【相關字彙與重要片語】

¹fear［fɪr］（n.）／（v.）恐懼 （phr.）①in fear of 怕 ②fear for 為……擔心

99．⁴atmosphere［ˈætməsˌfɪr］（n.）①大氣 ②空氣 ③氣氛

100．¹grow［gro］（v.）①成長；發育 ②增加 ③種植 （phr.）grow up 長大

【諺】Absence makes the heart <u>grow</u> fonder. 小別勝新婚。

²absence（n.）缺席 fonder（adj.）更喜愛的

101．¹go ¹from ¹bad ¹to ¹worse（phr.）愈來愈糟糕

102. ^{1}last ^{1}for（phr.）持續

103. ^{1}for ^{1}example（phr.）例如

　　【諺】Example is better than precept. 身教重於言教。

　　　　precept（n.）訓誡

104. ^{2}whenever [hwɛnˋɛvɚ]（adv.）每當

105. ^{1}come ^{1}back（phr.）回來

　　【諺】A bad penny always comes back. 惡有惡報。

　　　　^{3}penny（n.）（美）一分（硬幣）

106. ^{1}again ^{1}and ^{1}again（phr.）再三地

107. ^{1}do one's ^{1}best（phr.）全力以赴

108. ^{1}each ^{1}time（phr.）每次

109. ^{1}get ^{3}rid ^{1}of（phr.）擺脫

　　【相關字彙】

　　^{3}rid [rɪd]（v.）使免除

110. ^{3}frequent [ˋfrikwənt]（adj.）①時常發生的；屢次的 ②習以
　　為常的 （v.）時常出入於

　　【相關字彙】

　　^{4}frequency [ˋfrikwənsɪ]（n.）頻繁；頻率

111. ^{4}continuous [kənˋtɪnjuəs]（adj.）繼續的；連續的

112. reappearance [ˌriəˋpɪrəns]（n.）再現

113. ^{1}ghost [gost]（n.）幽靈；鬼

114. ^{6}thereafter [ðɛrˋæftɚ]（adv.）之後；以後

115. ^{1}as ^{1}soon ^{1}as（phr.）一……就

116. ²wake ¹up（phr.）①醒來 ②醒悟

【相關字彙】

²wake [wek]（v.）醒來；喚醒

117. startled [ˋstɑrtḷd]（adj.）受驚嚇的

【相關字彙與重要片語】

⁵startle [ˋstɑrtḷ]（v.）使驚嚇；使驚奇 （phr.）be startled at 給……嚇一跳

118. ³scream [skrim]（v.）/（n.）尖叫（聲）

119. loudly [ˋlaʊdlɪ]（adv.）大聲地

【相關字彙與重要片語】

¹loud [laʊd]（adj.）大聲的 （phr.）out loud 出聲；大聲地

120. ⁶anticipate [ænˋtɪsəˌpet]（v.）預期；期待

【相關字彙】

⁶anticipation [ænˌtɪsəˋpeʃən]（n.）預期；預料

121. ¹in ¹front ¹of（phr.）在……的前面

122. ¹right ¹away（phr.）馬上

123. ¹cry ¹out（phr.）大叫

124. ³panic [ˋpænɪk]（n.）恐慌；驚慌

125. ⁵shiver ¹with ¹fear（phr.）嚇得發抖

【相關字彙】

⁵shiver [ˋʃɪvɚ]（v.）/（n.）顫抖

126. ³scary [ˋskɛrɪ]（adj.）嚇人的；可怕的

127. incomprehensible [ɪnˌkɑmprɪˋhɛnsəbḷ]（adj.）無法理解的

【相關字彙】

[5]comprehend [ˌkɑmprɪˈhɛnd]（v.）理解；領悟

128. [1]happen [ˈhæpən]（v.）①發生 ②偶然；碰巧

129. succumb [1]to（phr.）屈服於

130. [3]nervous [6]breakdown（phr.）精神崩潰

【相關字彙】

[3]nerve [nɝv]（n.）①神經 ②神經過敏 ③勇敢；魄力

[3]nervous [ˈnɝvəs]（adj.）①緊張的 ②神經（質）的

[6]breakdown [ˈbrekˌdaʊn]（n.）①故障 ②崩潰

131. [5]rifle [ˈraɪfl]（n.）來福槍；步槍

132. crazily [ˈkrezɪlɪ]（adv.）瘋狂地

【相關字彙】

[2]crazy [ˈkrezɪ]（adj.）①瘋狂的 ②狂熱的；熱衷的

133. [2]shoot [ʃut]（v.）①射中；射殺 ②開槍 ③發射 （n.）① 射擊 ②拍攝 （phr.）shoot a film 拍攝影片

134. [1]for [1]seconds（phr.）幾秒鐘

135. [6]hysterical [hɪsˈtɛrɪkl]（adj.）歇斯底里的

136. [1]cut Sb.'s [1]body [1]into [1]pieces（phr.）將某人分屍

【相關字彙與重要片語】

[1]cut [kʌt]（v.）切；割；剪；砍 （phr.）a short cut 捷徑

【諺】The tongue is not steel, yet it cuts.

舌雖非利刃，卻可傷人。 [2]tongue（n.）舌頭

[2]steel（n.）鋼；刀

137. ¹different [ˈdɪfərənt]（adj.）①<u>不同的</u> ②各別的 （phr.）be different from 與……不同

【相關字彙與重要片語】

²difference [ˈdɪfərəns]（n.）不同；差異 （phr.）with a difference 引人注目；與眾不同

138. satisfied [ˈsætɪsˌfaɪd]（adj）感到滿意的

【相關字彙與重要片語】

²satisfy [ˈsætɪsˌfaɪ]（v.）使滿足 （phr.）be satisfied with 滿意

⁴satisfaction [ˌsætɪsˈfækʃən]（n.）滿足

139. ¹write ¹down（phr.）把……寫下

140. ¹page [pedʒ]（n.）頁 （phr.）①front page 報紙頭版 ②page-turner 令人欲罷不能的書

141. ²diary [ˈdaɪərɪ]（n.）日記 （phr.）keep a diary 每天寫日記

142. finished [ˈfɪnɪʃt]（adj.）完蛋了的

143. ¹go ¹to ¹bed（phr.）上床睡覺

144. ¹worry [ˈwɝɪ]（v.）憂慮；擔心 （n.）<u>令人發愁的事（或人）</u> （phr.）worry about 擔心

145. ¹at midnight（phr.）在半夜

【相關字彙與重要片語】

midnight [ˈmɪdˌnaɪt]（n.）/（adj.）午夜（的） （phr.）burn the midnight oil 熬夜；開夜車

146. suddenly [ˈsʌdn̩lɪ]（adv.）突然地

【相關字彙】

²sudden [ˋsʌdn̩]（adj.）忽然的；突然的

147. ²forgive [fəˋgɪv]（v.）原諒；寬恕

148. finally [ˋfaɪn̩lɪ]（adv.）最終地；最後地

【相關字彙】

¹final [ˋfaɪn̩]（adj.）①最終的；最後的 ②決定性的；終極的（n.）①決賽 ②期末考

149. ⁴commit ³suicide（phr.）自殺

【相關字彙】

⁴commit [kəˋmɪt]（v.）①做（錯事）；犯（罪）②使作出保證

³suicide [ˋsuəˏsaɪd]（n.）自殺

150. ¹a ¹few（phr.）一些

151. ⁴rescue [ˋrɛskju]（v.）/（n.）援救

152. ¹discover [dɪsˋkʌvə]（v.）發現

【相關字彙】

³discovery [dɪsˋkʌvərɪ]（n.）發現

153. gunshot [ˋgʌnˏʃɑt]（n.）射擊

154. ¹according ¹to（phr.）根據；依照

155. ²expert [ˋɛkspɜt]（n.）專家 （adj.）熟練的；專家的

【相關字彙】

⁶expertise [ˏɛkspəˋtiz]（n.）①專門知識；專門技術 ②專家鑑定

156. ^{6}assumption [ə`sʌmpʃən]（n.）假定；假設

【相關字彙】

^{4}assume [ə`sjum]（v.）①認爲；臆測 ②負起（責任或任務） ③假裝

157. ^{2}consider [kən`sɪdə]（v.）①熟慮；考慮 ②視爲；認爲

158. ^{1}because ^{1}of（phr.）由於；因爲

159. illness [`ɪlnɪs]（n.）疾病

【相關字彙與重要片語】

^{2}ill [ɪl]（adj.）①生病的 ②壞的 （phr.）speak ill of 講……的壞話

160. ^{4}furthermore [`fɝðə`mor]（adv.）而且；此外；再者

161. ^{2}main [men]（adj.）主要的

162. ^{1}cause [kɔz]（n.）原因 （v.）①引起；帶來 ②使某人做某事

163. absolutely [`æbsəlutlɪ]（adv.）絕對地；完全地

【相關字彙】

^{4}absolute [`æbsəlut]（adj.）絕對的；完全的

164. ^{1}point ^{1}out（phr.）指出

165. strangely [`strendʒlɪ]（adv.）奇怪地；奇妙地

【相關字彙】

^{1}strange [strendʒ]（adj.）①奇怪的 ②陌生的 ③不習慣的

166. ^{3}mention [`mɛnʃən]（v.）提及；說到；寫到 （phr.）at the mention of 當說到

167. ¹show ¹up（phr.）出現

168. endlessly [ˈɛndləslɪ]（adv.）無止盡地

169. ⁶illusion [ɪˈluʒən]（n.）幻覺；錯覺

170. ²experience [ɪkˈspɪrɪəns]（n.）/（v.）經驗；遭受

171. madness [ˈmædnɪs]（n.）瘋狂

　　【相關字彙與重要片語】

　　¹mad [mæd]（adj.）①激動的；瘋狂的 ②生氣的 （phr.）
　　mad at 生氣

172. ¹possible [ˈpɑsəbl̩]（adj.）可能的

173. ⁴psychologist [saɪˈkɑlədʒɪst]（n.）心理學家

174. ¹out ¹of（phr.）①出於 ②用光

175. loneliness [ˈlonlɪnɪs]（n.）寂寞

176. sleepwalk [ˈslipˌwɔk]（v.）/（n.）夢遊

177. ¹dig ¹up（phr.）掘起

　　【相關字彙】

　　¹dig [dɪg]（v.）①挖掘 ②發掘；探究

178. ¹move [muv]（v.）①搬動；移動 ②感動 （n.）搬動；移
　　動 （phr.）get a move on 趕快

179. ¹be ³aware ¹of（phr.）知道

　　【相關字彙】

　　³aware [əˈwɛr]（adj.）注意到；知道

180. ⁶bizarre [bɪˈzɑr]（adj.）奇異的；異乎尋常的

181. ⁴behavior [bɪˈhevjɚ]（n.）行為；舉止

～ 第二章 ～
惡夢

有一本神祕的（⁴mysterious）日記，曾經在大約十年前的一份當地的（²local）報紙上被報導過。日記是被一位彼得・安德森先生，在他後面院子（²yard）的地底下（underground）發現。他是在美國密西根（Michigan）州（¹State），一位為私人的（²private）家庭工作的家庭教師（³tutor）。日記中敘述（⁶narrate）了一個關於一個家庭很可怕的惡夢（⁴nightmare）般的經歷。日記在第一頁非常開頭處訴說著：「很久以前，大約是在五十年前，在密西根州有一家十分和樂的四口人。他們是爸爸，約翰、媽媽，琳達，和他們的兩個女兒。較年長的（²elder）女兒叫做莎拉，而蘿絲則是小女兒。約翰先生非常熱愛（⁵adore）他的家庭。他的女兒莎拉達到（¹reach）了成年期（⁵adulthood）。但是，蘿絲很年幼，年齡六歲。小小的蘿絲對她的家人而言，就像是一位天

⟡ Chapter 2 ⟡
The Nightmare

There was a [1]mysterious diary once reported in a [2]local newspaper about ten years ago. The diary was found [3]underground by Mr. Peter Anderson in his back [4]yard. He was a [5]tutor [6]working for a [7]private family in the [8]State of [9]Michigan, USA. The diary [10]narrated a very scary [11]nightmare about one family. It said [12]in the very beginning on the first page: "[13]Once upon a time, about fifty years ago, there was a very happy family of four people in Michigan. They were Father, John, Mother, Linda, and their two daughters. The [14]elder daughter was Sarah, and Rose was the little one. Mr. John [15]adored his family a lot. The daughter, Sarah, had just [16]reached [17]adulthood. But Rose was very young [18]at the age of six. Little Rose was like an [19]angel to her family." The [20]horrible story about this happy

使（³angel）。」這個關於此快樂的家庭可怕的（³horrible）故事，是像以下這樣開始的。

　　整家人事先計畫好，他們要去密西根州北部地區。一個靠近美麗的蘇必略湖的地方。他們將會在一個空閒的週末去那邊四周露營。那裡的湖水是湛藍、深邃與透明的（⁵transparent），有時在湖面上有船航行著。其中，最特別的部分是：人們能看見鄰近（²nearby）那著名的、美麗的、黃顏色的瀑布（²waterfall），被稱呼（¹call）爲塔括門濃瀑布。瀑布顏色上看起來如同琥珀（amber）一般。瀑布充滿著豐富（⁵abundant）數量（²amount）的鐵質（¹iron）。此外，在瀑布旁邊（¹beside），很多人們悠閒地（⁴leisurely）在湖上用槳划船（⁵paddle）著，並貪婪地（greedily）享受（²enjoy）著他們所需要的儘可能多的美好（²lovely）陽光。湖泊中常常充滿著豐富的魚群。當很多人小酌一番那濃郁、香醇的（⁶mellow）啤酒（²beer）時，他們喜歡試一試一些那油炸的（fried）、美味的（²delicious）白魚。

family went [21]as follows.

The whole family planned [22]in advance to go to the northern area in Michigan. It was [23]close to beautiful [24]Lake Superior. They would [25]go camping on a free weekend around there. The water was blue, deep, and [26]transparent there with ships sailing on the lake sometimes. One of the most special parts was that people could also see the famous, beautiful, and yellow-colored [27]waterfalls [28]nearby. They were [29]called the Tahquamenon Falls. It looked like [30]amber in color. The falls were [31]filled with [32]abundant [33]amounts of [34]iron. [35]Beside the waterfalls, many people [36]paddled boats [37]leisurely on the lake and [38]greedily [39]enjoyed the [40]lovely sunshine they needed [41]as much as possible. The lake often [42]abounded with [43]schools of fish. When people drank that rich and [44]mellow [45]beer, they liked to try some [46]fried and [47]delicious Whitefish.

一天，全家到達（³arrival）露營區，整家人就在之後立即（²upon）卸下（unload）了行李（³luggage），而接著使他們自己十分忙碌（⁴occupy）搭起帳篷。他們開始搭起他們手邊有的帳篷，並享受在荒野（²wild）中稀有的（²rare）一頓野餐大餐（²meal）。在第一天晚上，當整家人坐著圍繞一個大營火（campfire）時，他們高興地唱歌、跳舞，和彼此交換（³exchange）說著使人愉悅的（entertaining）故事。然後，禿頭（⁴bald）了的父親站起身來，彈奏起他的舊吉他。這把吉他是在一場拍賣（⁶auction）上購買來的。他臉紅（⁴blush）著，並且溫柔地（tenderly）對著坐在他身旁的母親唱著，在他們年輕的時候，過去當他們如同男女朋友正在約會（¹date）的時候對她唱的那些深情的（⁶sentimental）情歌。彈奏完畢，在掌聲（⁵applause）之中（⁴amid）爸爸坐到長椅（²bench）上。準備（¹prepare）睡覺之前，他們拍了一張全家福的照片來紀念（⁶commemorate）這一個美好的（²wonderful）露營夜晚。

One day, [48]upon their [49]arrival at the [50]camping grounds, the whole family [51]unloaded their [52]luggage and then [53]occupied themselves [54]setting up camp. They began to [55]put up the tents that they had [56]at hand and enjoyed a [57]rare big picnic [58]meal in the [59]wild. On the first night, the whole family sat around a big [60]campfire, singing happily, dancing, and [61]exchanging [62]entertaining stories with each other. Then, the [63]bald father stood up and played his old guitar. His guitar was bought at an [64]auction. He [65]blushed and sang [66]tenderly to the mother, sitting beside him, those [67]sentimental love songs he had once sung to her [68]in their youth, when they had been [69]dating as boyfriend and girlfriend. After playing, the father sat down on a [70]bench [71]amid [72]applause. Before [73]preparing to sleep, they [74]took a family photo to [75]commemorate the [76]wonderful camp night.

　　這時，小女兒蘿絲，突然開始氣喘（⁶asthma）發作（²attack）而不舒服起來。約翰先生心裡想著：「她是對圍繞營區這裡的些許花粉（pollen）過敏嗎？」爸爸趕緊（⁴hasten）求救，並且幫忙他女兒做（³perform）必要的（²necessary）心肺復甦術。然而，這名小女孩未能有充分的（¹enough）時間去附近的醫院接受緊急（³emergency）的治療（²treatment）。很快地，她停止了呼吸（³breathe）。她緊接地（immediately）倒地而死去。沒有任何人能使她甦醒（⁵revive）過來。

　　在那時候，這不幸的事件（⁴incident），無意地（unintentionally）被營區另一邊的一位陌生人（²stranger）使用攝影機（camcorder）錄製（²record）了下來。當警察與醫療的（³medical）人員（³staff）到達時，他們全部看到了在錄影機裡中的景象（¹scene），而使他們驚嚇（²frighten）不已。結果，實際上是如此的。他們看到了一些在黑暗（darkness）之中模糊的（blurred）影像（³image）。小女孩蘿絲，站在靠近家人的

[77]At this point, the little daughter, Rose, suddenly began [78]suffering from an [79]attack of [80]asthma. "Is she [81]allergic to some [82]pollen around the camping grounds here?" thought Mr. John. The father [83]hastened to [84]call for help and [85]performed CPR on his daughter as [86]necessary. But the little girl did not have [87]enough time to go to the hospital nearby for [88]emergency [89]treatment. Soon she stopped [90]breathing. She [91]immediately [92]fell down to the ground and died. Nobody could [93]revive her.

[94]At that time, this unfortunate [95]incident was [96]unintentionally [97]recorded by a [98]stranger using a [99]camcorder on another side of the camping grounds. As the police and [100]medical [101]staff arrived, they all saw the [102]scene in the camcorder, and it [103]frightened them very much. It actually ended like this. They saw some [104]blurred [105]images amidst the [106]darkness. The little girl, Rose, stood near the back of the

帳篷後面。不清楚何時這樣的事發生了，則是從帳篷右邊看過去，一個人能模糊地（vaguely）看到一隻沾滿鮮血的（¹blood-stained）手，從他們的帳篷裡伸出來，彷彿緊緊地（firmly）掐（⁵pinch）住了小女孩脖子直到她死亡為止。

後來，這傷心的一家人返回（¹return）家後，經由這對雙親小心的（¹careful）調查（⁴investigation），過去殘酷的（²cruel）歷史（¹history）才被有所證實（²confirm）。遠古的（²ancient）時代（¹times），在那營地有一些本土的（³native）印地安種族（³tribe）曾經遭受到被白人屠殺（⁵slaughter）。

family's tent. It was not clear when this happened, but from the right side of the tent, one could [107]vaguely see that there was a [108]blood-stained hand [109]coming out of their tent [110]as if to [111]firmly [112]pinch the little girl's neck until she died.

[113]Later on, after the sad family [114]returned home, through the parents' [115]careful [116]investigations, the [117]cruel [118]history of the past was [119]confirmed. In [120]ancient [121]times, some [122]native Indian [123]tribes had once been [124]slaughtered by white people in the camp grounds.

Chapter 2

Vocabulary

1. ⁴mysterious [mɪsˋtɪrɪəs]（adj.）神祕的；不可思議的

2. ²local [ˋlokḷ]（adj.）①地方的；當地的 ②鄉土的 （n.）本地人 （phr.）local call 本地電話；市內電話

3. underground [ˏʌndɚˋgraund]（adv.）地面下

4. ²yard [jɑrd]（n.）①碼（英美長度單位） ②<u>庭院；院子</u>
   【諺】Give him an inch and he'll take a <u>yard</u>. 得寸進尺。
   ¹inch（n.）英吋

5. ³tutor [ˋtjutɚ]（n.）<u>家庭教師</u> （v.）①當家庭教師 ②指導

6. ¹work ¹for（phr.） 為……工作

7. ²private [ˋpraɪvɪt]（adj.）①私立的 ②<u>私人的</u> （phr.）in private 私下
   【相關字彙】
   ⁴privacy [ˋpraɪvəsɪ]（n.）隱私（權）

8. ¹state [stet]（n.）①狀態；情況 ②國家 ③（常大寫）<u>美國的州</u> （v.）陳述；說明
   【相關字彙】
   ²statement [ˋstetmənt]（n.）（正式的）聲明
   ⁵statesman [ˋstetsmən]（n.）政治家

9. Michigan [ˋmɪʃəgən] 密西根州（美國州名）

10. ⁶narrate [næˈret]（v.）敘述；說明

　　【相關字彙】

　　⁶narrative [ˈnærətɪv]（n.）敘述；故事

　　⁶narrator [næˈretɚ]（n.）敘述者；說明者

11. ⁴nightmare [ˈnaɪt͵mɛr]（n.）惡夢

12. ¹in ¹the ¹very beginning（phr.）最開始

13. ¹once ²upon ¹a ¹time（phr.）從前

14. ²elder [ˈɛldɚ]（adj.）①年紀較長的 ②地位高的 （n.）①年長的人 ②前輩

15. ⁵adore [əˈdor]（v.）①崇拜 ②熱愛

16. ¹reach [ritʃ]（v.）①達到；到達 ②伸手及到 ③與……取得聯繫 （n.）可觸及的範圍 （phr.）①reach for 伸手去拿 ②beyond Sb.'s reach 某人搆不到的；力所不及的

17. ⁵adulthood [əˈdʌlthʊd]（n.）成年（期）

　　【相關字彙】

　　¹adult [əˈdʌlt]（n.）大人；成人 （adj.）成人的

18. ¹at ¹the ¹age ¹of（phr.）幾歲時

　　【相關字彙與重要片語】

　　¹age [edʒ]（n.）①年齡 ②（常大寫）年代 （v.）變老 （phr.）①be of age 成年 ②come of age 到達法定年齡 ③under age 未成年

19. ³angel [ˈendʒəl]（n.）天使；天使般的人

20. ³horrible [ˈhɔrəbl]（adj.）①恐怖的；可怕的 ②極討厭的

21. ¹as follows（phr.）如下

【相關字彙與重要片語】

¹follow [ˈfɑlo]（v.）①跟隨　②接著　③聽從　（phr.）¹follow the fashion 趕時髦　②follow one's nose 筆直走；按本能行事 ☆ ³fashion（n.）時尚

22. ¹in ²advance（phr.）事先

【相關字彙】

²advance [ədˈvæns]（n.）/（v.）前進；發展　（adj.）預先的；事先的

23. ¹be ¹close ¹to（phr.）靠近

24. ¹Lake ³Superior（phr.）蘇必略湖（北美五大湖之一）

【相關字彙】

³superior [səˈpɪrɪə]（adj.）卓越的；優秀的　（n.）①優秀的人　②長官；上司

25. ¹go caming（phr.）露營

【相關字彙】

¹camp [kæmp]（n.）/（v.）①露營　②野營；營地

26. ⁵transparent [trænsˈpɛrənt]（adj.）①透明的　②明顯的

27. ²waterfall [ˈwɔtəˌfɔl]（n.）瀑布

28. ²nearby [ˈnɪrˌbaɪ]（adj.）附近的

29. ¹call [kɔl]（v.）①呼叫　②稱呼；取名　③打電話　（phr.）①call on 拜訪　②call Sb. back 回某人電話

【諺】The pot called the kettle black. 五十步笑百步。

²pot（n.）鍋子　³kettle（n.）水壺

30. amber [`æmbɚ]（n.）琥珀

31. ¹be ¹filled ¹with（phr.）使充滿

【相關字彙與重要片語】

¹fill [fɪl]（v.）使充滿；填滿　（phr.）①fill out 填寫 ②fill Sb.'s shoes 接替某人

32. ⁵abundant [ə`bʌndənt]（adj.）豐富的；富足的

33. ²amount [ə`maʊnt]（n.）①<u>數量</u> ②（金錢）總額　（v.）總計　（phr.）amount to 總計

34. ¹iron [`aɪɚn]（n.）①<u>鐵</u> ②熨斗　（adj.）①鐵製的 ②剛強的

【諺】Strike while the <u>iron</u> is hot. 打鐵趁熱。

　　　²strike（v.）打；擊

35. ¹beside [bɪ`saɪd]（prep.）①<u>在……旁邊</u> ②與……無關　（phr.）①beside the question 與問題無關 ②beside oneself 極度興奮

36. ⁵paddle [`pædl]（n.）（寬的）槳　（v.）<u>用槳划船</u>

37. ⁴leisurely [`liʒɚlɪ]（adj.）/（adv.）<u>匆容不迫的（地）；悠閒的（地）</u>

【相關字彙】

³leisure [`liʒɚ]（n.）閒暇；空閒

38. greedily [`gridɪlɪ]（adv.）貪婪地

【相關字彙】

²greedy [`gridɪ]（adj.）①貪婪的；貪心的 ②貪吃的；嘴饞的

⁵greed [grid]（n.）貪婪

39. ²enjoy [ɪnˋdʒɔɪ]（v.）享受；喜愛 （phr.）enjoy oneself 過得快活

40. ²lovely [ˋlʌvlɪ]（adj.）①可愛的 ②美好的；令人愉快的

41. ¹as ⋯¹as ¹possible（phr.）儘可能

42. ⁶abound ¹with（phr.）充滿

【相關字彙與重要片語】

⁶abound [əˋbaʊnd]（v.）①充滿；充足 ②富足 （phr.）abound in 富於

43. ¹school ¹of（phr.）（魚）群

44. ⁶mellow [ˋmɛlo]（adj.）①（聲音）圓潤的 ②（酒）芳醇的

45. ²beer [bɪr]（n.）啤酒 （phr.）ginger beer 薑汁啤酒
☆ ⁴ginger（n.）薑

46. fried [fraɪd]（adj.）油炸的

【相關字彙與重要片語】

³fry [fraɪ]（v.）油炸；油煎；油炒 （phr.）French fries 炸薯條

47. ²delicious [dɪˋlɪʃəs]（adj.）美味的

48. ²upon [əˋpɑn]（prep.）①在⋯⋯上面 ②在⋯⋯（之）後立即

49. ³arrival [əˋraɪvl]（n.）①到達 ②抵達的人（或事物）

【相關字彙】

²arrive [əˋraɪv]（v.）到達

50. ¹camping ¹ground（phr.）野營營地

51. unload [ʌnˋlod] (v.) 卸（貨）

52. ³luggage [ˋlʌgɪdʒ] (n.) 行李

53. ⁴occupy [ˋɑkjəˏpaɪ] (v.) ①佔領 ②佔用 ③使忙碌 （phr.）
    occupy oneself with 忙碌於
    【相關字彙】
    ⁴occupation [ˏɑkjəˋpeʃən] (n.) ①職業 ②佔領

54. ¹set ¹up ¹camp（phr.）搭帳篷

55. ¹put ¹up ¹the ²tent（phr.）搭帳篷
    【相關字彙】
    ²tent [tɛnt] (n.) 帳篷

56. ¹at ¹hand（phr.）手邊

57. ²rare [rɛr] (adj.) ①珍奇的；稀罕的 ②（肉等）半熟的；
    半生不熟的

58. ²meal [mil] (n.) 一餐

59. ²wild [waɪld] (n.) 荒野 （adj.）①野生的 ②荒涼的 ③野
    蠻的

60. campfire [ˋkæmpˏfaɪr] (n.) 營火

61. ³exchange [ɪksˋtʃendʒ] (n.) ／ (v.) ①兌換 ②交換

62. entertaining [ˏɛntəˋtenɪŋ] (adj.) 使人愉悅的；有趣的
    【相關字彙】
    ⁴entertain [ˏɛntəˋten] (v.) ①使娛樂 ②款待；招待
    ⁴entertainment [ˏɛntəˋtenmənt] (n.) ①娛樂 ②款待；招待

63. ⁴bald [bɔld] (adj.) ①禿頭的 ②（植物）無葉的；（動物）

無毛的　③露骨的

64. ⁶auction [ˋɔkʃən]（v.）/（n.）拍賣

65. ⁴blush [blʌʃ]（v.）/（n.）臉紅

66. tenderly [ˋtɛndəlɪ]（adv.）溫柔地

【相關字彙】

³tender [ˋtɛndə]（adj.）①溫柔的　②嫩的　③脆弱的

67. ⁶sentimental [ˌsɛntəˋmɛntl̩]（adj.）深情的；多愁善感的

68. ¹in one's ²youth（phr.）某人年輕時期

【相關字彙與重要片語】

²youth [juθ]（n.）年青；青春　（phr.）youth hostel 青年旅社　☆ ⁴hostel 旅社

69. ¹date [det]（v.）①約會　②註明日期　（n.）①日期　②約會；約會對象　③時期；年代　（phr.）①up to date 最新的；新式的　②out of date　過時的

70. ²bench [bɛntʃ]（n.）長凳；長椅

71. ⁴amid/⁴amidst [əˋmɪd]/[əˋmɪdst]（prep.）在……之中

72. ⁵applause [əˋplɔz]（n.）掌聲；稱讚

【相關字彙】

⁵applaud [əˋplɔd]（v.）鼓掌叫好

73. ¹prepare [prɪˋpɛr]（v.）①準備；預備　②做成（飯菜）（phr.）prepare for 為……作準備

【相關字彙】

³preparation [ˌprɛpəˋreʃən]（n.）準備；預備

74. ¹take ¹a ¹family ²photo（phr.）照全家福相片

　　【相關字彙】

　　²photo [ˋfoto]（n.）照片　（v.）照相

75. ⁶commemorate [kəˋmɛməˏret]（v.）慶祝；紀念

76. ²wonderful [ˋwʌndəfəl]（adj.）①令人驚奇的 ②美好的

77. ¹at ¹this ¹point（phr.）此時

78. ³suffer ¹from（phr.）遭受……痛苦

　　【相關字彙】

　　³suffer [ˋsʌfə]（v.）①遭受 ②忍受 ③罹患

79. ²attack [əˋtæk]（v.）攻擊　（n.）①攻擊 ②發作；害病

80. ⁶asthma [ˋæzmə]（n.）氣喘（病）；哮喘

81. ¹be ⁵allergic ¹to（phr.）對……過敏

　　【相關字彙】

　　⁵allergic [əˋlɝdʒɪk]（adj.）①過敏的 ②對……極討厭的

　　⁵allergy [ˋælədʒɪ]（n.）①過敏症 ②厭惡；反感

82. pollen [ˋpɑlən]（n.）花粉

83. ⁴hasten [ˋhesn̩]（v.）趕緊；催促

84. ¹call ¹for ¹help（phr.）求救

　　【相關字彙與重要片語】

　　¹help [hɛlp]（v.）①幫忙 ②促進 ③治療　（phr.）①help
　　Sb. out 幫忙某人 ②help Sb. with St. 幫助某人某事

　　²helpful [ˋhɛlpfəl]（adj.）有益的；有幫助的　（phr.）be
　　helpful to Sb. 對某人有幫助

85. ³perform [pɚˋfɔrm]（v.）①做；完成 ②上演

86. ²necessary [ˋnɛsəˏsɛrɪ]（adj.）必要的；必須的

87. ¹enough [əˋnʌf]（adj.）足夠的

88. ³emergency [ɪˋmɝdʒənsɪ]（n.）緊急事件 （phr.）in an emergency 在緊要關頭

89. ²treatment [ˋtritmənt]（n.）①待遇；對待 ②處理 ③治療 （法）

【相關字彙與重要片語】

²treat [trit]（v.）/（n.）①對待 ②請客 ③處理 （phr.） trick or treat（萬聖節用語）不給糖就搗蛋

90. ³breathe [brið]（v.）呼吸

【相關字彙與重要片語】

³breath [brɛθ]（n.）呼吸 （phr.）a foul breath 口臭

☆ ⁵foul （adj.）惡臭的

91. immediately [ɪˋmidɪɪtlɪ]（adv.）立即地；馬上地

【相關字彙】

³immediate [ɪˋmidɪɪt]（adj.）①即刻的；立刻的 ②目前的

92. ¹fall ¹down（phr.）倒下

【相關字彙與重要片語】

¹fall [fɔl]（n.）①（美）秋天 ②瀑布 ③墮落 （v.）① 落下；降落 ②倒下；跌倒 ③下降；減弱 （phr.）①fall behind 落後 ②fall through 失敗 ③fall/land/drop on one's feet 化險為夷；運氣好

【諺】United we stand；divided we fall.

團結即存，分裂即亡。

³unite（v.）團結　²divide（v.）分

93. ⁵revive [rɪ'vaɪv]（v.）①使甦醒 ②使重新流行

94. ¹at ¹that ¹time（phr.）在那時候

95. ⁴incident ['ɪnsədn̩t]（n.）事件

96. unintentionally [ˌʌnɪn'tɛnʃənlɪ]（adv.）非故意地

97. ²record ['rɛkəd]（n.）①唱片 ②記錄 （phr.）①break the record 破記錄 ②keep in record 被記載

　　　　　 ＊ [rɪ'kɔrd]（v.）①記錄 ②錄製

98. ²stranger ['strendʒə]（n.）①陌生人 ②異鄉人

99. camcorder ['kæmˌkɔrdə]（n.）手提錄音攝影機

100. ³medical ['mɛdɪkl̩]（adj.）醫學的；醫療的

　　　【相關字彙】

　　　²medicine ['mɛdəsn̩]（n.）①醫學；醫術 ②藥物；內服藥

　　　⁶medication [ˌmɛdɪ'keʃən]（n.）藥物治療

101. ³staff [stæf]（n.）①（全體）工作人員 ②杖；棒；棍

102. ¹scene [sin]（n.）①景色；景象 ②（出事）地點；現場 （phr.）behind the scenes ①在後臺 ②祕密地

　　　【相關字彙】

　　　⁴scenery ['sinərɪ]（n.）風景；景色

　　　⁶scenic ['sinɪk]（adj.）風景的

103. ²frighten ['fraɪtn̩]（v.）①使害怕；使驚恐 ②嚇唬某人使其

做某事

104. blurred [bl3d]（adj.）模糊的；難辨別的

　　【相關字彙】

　　⁵blur [bl3]（v.）使模糊；使朦朧　　（n.）汙點

105. ³image [`ɪmɪdʒ]（n.）①雕像；肖像　②影像　③形象；印象

　　（phr.）self-image　自我形象

106. darkness [`dɑrknɪs]（n.）黑暗

107. vaguely [`veglɪ]（adv.）不清晰地；模糊地

　　【相關字彙】

　　⁵vague [veg]（adj.）模糊的；含糊的

108. ¹blood-stained [`blʌd`stend]（adj.）血玷污的

　　【相關字彙與重要片語】

　　¹blood [blʌd]（n.）①血液　②血統；家世　　（phr.）①blood
　　type（醫）血型　②fresh/new blood 新成員　③blood donation
　　捐血　☆ ⁶donation（n.）捐贈；捐款

　　【諺】<u>Blood</u> is thicker than water. 血濃於水。

　　　　²thick（adj.）濃厚的

　　stained [stend]（adj.）玷污的

　　⁵stain [sten]（v.）染污　（n.）污點

109. ¹come ¹out（phr.）出現

110. ¹as ¹if（phr.）彷彿

111. firmly [`f3mlɪ]（adv.）①堅固地；牢牢地　②堅定地

　　【相關字彙與重要片語】

²firm ［fɝm］（adj.）①堅固的；堅實地 ②堅定的；堅決的
（n.）公司；商行 （phr.）stand firm 堅定不移；不讓步

112. ⁵pinch ［pɪntʃ］（v.）<u>捏；掐；擰；夾</u>（n.）①捏；掐；擰；
夾 ②（一）撮；少量 （phr.）in a pinch 在緊急關頭

113. later ¹on （phr.）稍後

114. ¹return ［rɪˋtɝn］（v.）/（n.）①<u>返回</u> ②歸還 （phr.）①
（英）return ticket 往返票 ②make a return for 報答 ③in
return for 酬謝

115. ¹careful ［ˋkɛrfəl］（adj.）謹慎的；小心的 （phr.）careful with
money 不亂花錢

116. ⁴investigation ［ɪn‚vɛstəˋgeʃən］（n.）調查；研究
【相關字彙】
³investigate ［ɪnˋvɛstə‚get］（v.）調查；研究

117. ²cruel ［ˋkruəl］（adj.）殘酷的；殘忍的
【相關字彙】
⁴cruelty ［ˋkruəltɪ］（n.）殘酷；殘忍

118. ¹history ［ˋhɪstərɪ］（n.）①<u>歷史</u> ②履歷；經歷；病歷
（phr.）life history 生平
【諺】<u>History</u> repeats itself. 歷史重演。
²repeat（v.）重複

119. ²confirm ［kənˋfɝm］（v.）①<u>證實</u> ②增強

120. ²ancient ［ˋenʃənt］（adj.）古代的；遠古的

121. ¹times ［taɪmz］（n.）時代；年代

122. ³native ['netɪv] (adj.) ①.本土的；本國的 ②自然的；天賦的 ③原產的 (n.) 本地人 (phr.) ①native speaker 說母語者 ②native American 印地安人（的）

123. ³tribe [traɪb] (n.) 種族；部落

124. ⁵slaughter ['slɔtɚ] (n.) /（v.) 屠殺；屠宰

❧ 第三章 ❧

夜遊

據說在兩年前，有一群大膽的（daring），而且有男子氣概的（⁵masculine）青少年（²teenager），總共五個人，他們平均的（³average）年齡為十七歲。他們時常覺得很無聊（bored），所以感到好似必須做不一樣的事情。他們想要得到一些刺激（²excitement），來改變他們所居住鄉間（²countryside）的小村莊（²village）裡無聊的（boring）生活。有一天，半夜裡無意上床睡覺，他們一起開了一輛車到很遙遠的一個地方，在台灣（Taiwan）台中縣的荒郊野外（⁵wilderness）。這些青少年彼此在個性（³personality）上，都有一樣的共同點：他們之中沒有一位會害怕像是鬼的事，而且當談論有關鬼怪時，甚至不會顯露出一點兒輕微（⁴slight）害怕的樣子。

∽ Chapter 3 ∽
The Night Drive

[1]It was said that two years ago, there was [2]a group of [3]daring and [4]masculine [5]teenagers, five [6]in total, whose [7]average age was seventeen. They often felt very [8]bored, so they felt like they needed to [9]do something different. They wanted to have some [10]excitement to change their [11]boring lives in the small [12]countryside [13]village where they lived. One day, not [14]willing to sleep, they drove a car together to a very far place in the [15]wilderness of [16]Taichung County, [17]Taiwan at midnight. These teenagers' [18]personalities all [19]had something in common with each other: none of them was [20]afraid of things like ghosts and did [21]not even show [22]a [23]slight bit of fear at all when [24]talking about ghosts.

那晚，在他們並無特定的（²particular）目的地（⁵destination）夜遊的路上，這群年輕人不斷地說著很無禮的（²rude）與粗俗的（⁶vulgar）關於死亡的笑話（¹joke）。此外（⁴moreover），他們全都笑（¹laugh）鬧地很大聲，並且，從他們不合宜的（improper）行為舉止中，你能看到他們最不（¹least）正經（decency）的樣子。甚至，當面向（¹face）著在路上兩旁的死者時，他們對死人和他們凌亂的（untidy）墳墓（⁴grave）顯露（¹show）出毫無任何尊敬（²respect）的樣子。他們有時非常不尊重地（disrespectfully）、輕率地（carelessly）指著那些死者的墓（⁴tomb），他們甚至對死者開起玩笑來。接著，突然他們開車開上去了一座很破舊的、紅色的拱（⁴arch）橋一會兒。這時，在完全的（²complete）黑暗之中，他們看到了什麼好像是有一名奇怪的女子，她的身上穿著白衣，為了搭他們的車子，正用她的兩隻手向他們揮手（²wave）。

That night, [25]on the way of their [26]night drive and not having a [27]particular [28]destination, the group of young people kept saying very [29]rude and [30]vulgar [31]jokes about death. [32]Moreover, they all [33]laughed very loudly, and from their [34]improper behavior, you could see they did not have the [35]least bit of [36]decency. Even when [37]facing the dead on both sides of the road, they [38]showed no [39]respect toward them and their [40]untidy [41]graves. They [42]pointed at those dead people's [43]tombs very [44]carelessly and [45]disrespectfully [46]at times ; they even joked about the dead. Then [47]all at once, they drove on a very old and red [48]arch bridge [49]for a while. At this time, in [50]complete darkness, they saw what seemed to be a strange woman, who was [51]dressed in white, [52]waving to them with both of her hands to [53]get a ride from them.

因此（²therefore），在所有人的同意（¹agreement）之下，車上的駕駛者，王偉，開始開車駛向這名女子所站住的方向（²direction）。他們正試著緩慢地接近（³approach）在他們前面的這個女人。然而（²however），黑暗中，過了一會兒，這名不知名的、一身是白的女子，好似漂浮（³float）著；卻不是站在地面之上。一位乘客（²passenger）名叫小優的女孩，坐在駕駛者旁邊，對於她所注意（¹notice）到的這可怕的情景尖叫（⁵shriek）了起來。她以告誡（warning）方式說著：「王偉！趕快把車開走！那個女人——啊！——好像沒有腳呀！」

此刻，每一個在車上的人都嚇壞了。王偉如此努力地嘗試很快踩（¹step）住油門（¹gas），加速（⁶accelerate）使車子移動地更快，以至於他能盡可能快地將車子開移逃離那名女（²female）鬼。符合了這些人的期待（³expectation），車子跑得更快了。但是，在他們逃亡期間，似乎那可怕的白衣女子，

[54]Therefore, [55]in accordance with everyone's [56]agreement, the driver, Wei Wang, started to drive the car in the [57]direction of where the woman stood. They were trying to [58]approach the woman in front of them slowly. [59]However, in the dark, [60]after a while, the unknown woman in white seemed to [61]float but not to stand above the ground. One [62]passenger, a girl, named Xiao-you, who was sitting [63]next to the driver, [64]shrieked at the scary scene which she [65]noticed. She said in [66]warning, "Wei Wang! Quickly drive the car away! That woman... uh...does not seem to have her feet!"

At this point, everybody in the car was [67]scared to death. Wei Wang tried hard to quickly [68]step on the [69]gas to [70]accelerate faster so that he could [71]get the car moving away from the [72]female ghost as soon as possible. To these people's [73]expectations, the car ran faster. But during their escape, it

她沒有眼球（eyeball），飛了起來，並且追趕（¹chase）在他們的車子後面，沒有她將會停止對他們所做的可怕行動的徵兆（²sign）。

最後，非常失望（⁵despair）之中，他們看到前面一條黑暗的小路（²path）上有絲毫（³trace）微弱的（³faint）光線（¹light）。驚訝地（surprisingly），有一所小間的警察局，在那裡被荒野圍繞住。所有的青少年，一等車子停止移動，就行動笨拙地（awkwardly）迅速地從車內跑出來。當從車子出來的時候，他們都無法平衡（³balance）好自己身體。他們全都從車子逃走（⁴flee）而跑向警察局。

在警察局裡，幾位人很好的員警非常熱心的（⁵enthusiastic），並且很注意聽著這群青少年盡力嘗試對他們解釋（²explain）的故事。這五名青少年一起告知警察，全部關

seemed that the scary woman in white, who had no [74]eyeballs, flew and [75]chased the back of their car. There were no [76]signs that she would stop her scary movement towards them.

Finally, through much [77]despair, they saw a [78]faint [79]trace of [80]light on a dark [81]path in front of them. [82]Surprisingly, there was a small police station there [83]surrounded by the wilderness. As soon as the car stopped moving, all of the teens [84]ran out of the car [85]in a hurry, moving [86]awkwardly. They couldn't [87]balance themselves very well while getting out of the car. They all [88]fled from the car and ran towards the police station.

In the police station, several nice policemen were very [89]enthusiastic and [90]paid [91]a lot of attention to the story which the group of teenagers [92]tried their best to [93]explain to them.

於剛才在路上稍早眞實地發生的事情。然而，過了一會兒，當中的一些青少年卻領悟（[2]realize）到一件更可怕的（frightful）事情。從這間小小的警局牆壁上所懸掛（[2]hang）著的一面大鏡子裡，青少年們並沒有看到任何警察們的映象（[3]shadow），證實（[1]prove）他們是存在（[3]existence）著。

The five teenagers told the police all about what had just really happened earlier on the road. However, after a bit, some of the teenagers [94]realized a more [95]frightful truth: from a large mirror [96]hanging on the wall in this small police station, the teenagers could not see any of the policemen's [97]shadows to [98]prove their [99]existence.

Chapter 3
Vocabulary

1. ¹it ¹is ¹said ¹that（phr.）據說

2. ¹a ¹group ¹of（phr.）一群

3. daring [ˋdɛrɪŋ]（adj.）大膽的

   【相關字彙】

   ³dare [dɛr]（v.）/（aux.）敢；膽敢

4. ⁵masculine [ˋmæskjəlɪn]（adj.）男性的；男子氣概的

5. ²teenager [ˋtinˏedʒɚ]（n.）十幾歲的青少年

   【相關字彙】

   ²teen [tin]（adj.）/（n.）十幾歲的（青少年）（指十三至十九歲）

   ²teenage [ˋtinˏedʒ]（adj.）十幾歲的

6. ¹in ¹total（phr.）總共

   【相關字彙】

   ¹total [ˋtotl]（adj.）①全體的；總計的 ②全然的；完全的（n.）/（v.）合計

7. ³average [ˋævərɪdʒ]（adj.）平均的 （n.）平均；普通 （v.）平均為

8. bored [bord]（adj.）感到無聊的

   【相關字彙與重要片語】

³bore ［bor］（v.）①使厭煩 ②鑽（孔）；鑿（井）；挖（通道）（n.）討厭的人（或事物）（phr.）be bored with 對……無聊（或厭煩）

⁵boredom ［ˋbordəm］（n.）無聊

9. ¹do ¹something ¹different（phr.）做不一樣的事

10. ²excitement ［ɪkˋsaɪtmənt］（n.）興奮；刺激（phr.）be excited about 對……興奮的

【相關字彙】

²excite ［ɪkˋsaɪt］（v.）①使興奮；使激動 ②引起；招致

11. boring ［ˋborɪŋ］（adj.）令人生厭的；無聊的

12. ²countryside ［ˋkʌntrɪˏsaɪd］（n.）鄉村；田園

【相關字彙】

¹country ［ˋkʌntrɪ］（n.）①國家 ②祖國；故鄉 ③鄉下

【諺】In the country of the blind, the one-eyed man is king.
比上不足，比下有餘。 ²blind（adj.）盲的

13. ²village ［ˋvɪlɪdʒ］（n.）村落；村莊

14. （¹be）²willing ¹to（phr.）有意願的；情願的

【相關字彙】

²willing ［ˋwɪlɪŋ］（adj.）情願的；願意的

15. ⁵wilderness ［ˋwɪldənɪs］（n.）荒野

16. Taichung ²County 台中縣（台灣地名）

【相關字彙】

²county ［ˋkaʊntɪ］（n.）縣（或郡）

17. Taiwan [ˈtaɪˈwɑn] 台灣

18. ³personality [ˌpɝsṇˈæləti]（n.）①<u>人格；個性</u> ②名人

    【相關字彙與重要片語】

    ¹person [ˈpɝsṇ]（n.）①人 ②身體；外表 ③（文法）人稱
    （phr.）in person 本人；親自

    ²personal [ˈpɝsṇḷ]（adj.）①個人的；私人的 ②本人的
    （n.）（報紙）人事消息欄

19. ¹have ¹something ¹in ¹common ¹with（phr.）與……有共同點

    【相關字彙與重要片語】

    ¹common [ˈkɑmən]（adj.）①共有的；公有的 ②普通的；
    常見的；平凡的 （phr.）common sense 常識

    ☆ ¹sense（n.）意識；概念

20. ¹be ¹afraid ¹of（phr.）恐怕；害怕

    【相關字彙】

    ¹afraid [əˈfred]（adj.）①恐懼的；害怕的 ②恐怕的；擔憂的

21. ¹not…¹at ¹all（phr.）一點也不

22. ¹a ¹bit ¹of（phr.）一點；有點

    【相關字彙】

    ¹bit [bɪt]（n.）①小片；小塊；小段 ②少量

23. ⁴slight [slaɪt]（adj.）輕微的；少許的

24. ¹talk ¹about（phr.）談論有關

25. ¹on ¹the ¹way（phr.）在途中

26. ¹night ¹drive（phr.）夜遊

27. ²particular [pəˋtɪkjələ] （adj.）①特定的；特別的 ②講究；挑剔 （phr.）①in particular尤其；特別 ②particular about 講究；挑剔

28. ⁵destination [ˌdɛstəˋneʃən] （n.）目的地

29. ²rude [rud] （adj.）無禮的；粗魯的

30. ⁶vulgar [ˋvʌlgə] （adj.）①粗俗的；粗鄙的 ②平民的；通俗的

31. ¹joke [dʒok] （n.）玩笑；笑話 （v.）開玩笑 （phr.）①crack/make a joke 開玩笑 ②play a joke on Sb. 戲弄某人；和某人開玩笑
    ☆ ⁴crack（v.）（口）說（笑話等）

32. ⁴moreover [morˋovə] （adv.）此外；並且

33. ¹laugh [læf] （v.）/（n.）笑 （phr.）laugh at 嘲笑
    【諺】Laugh and grow fat. 心寬體胖。

34. improper [ɪmˋprɑpə] （adj.）不適當的

35. ¹least [list] （adj.）/（adv.）/（n.）最少；最小；最不
    【諺】Least said, soonest mended. 言多必失；禍從口出
    ³mend（v.）修補；改善

36. decency [ˋdisn̩sɪ] （n.）（言語或舉止）正派；正經；得體
    【相關字彙】
    ⁶decent [ˋdisn̩t] （adj.）合宜的；正派的；端莊的

37. ¹face [fes] （v.）面臨；面向 （n.）①臉；面部 ②體面；面子 （phr.）①lose one's face 丟臉 ②have the face to do

竟有臉去做 ③set one's face not to do 下定決心不做

38. ¹show [ʃo] (v.) ①顯示；顯露 ②上映；演出 ③給……看 (n.) ①展覽會 ②表演；上演節目 ③賣弄 (phr.) ①talk show（電視、廣播電臺的）訪談節目；脫口秀 ②give/get Sb. a fair show 給某人以公平的機會 ③make a show of 賣弄

39. ²respect [rɪˈspɛkt] (n.) / (v.) 尊敬；尊重 (phr.) in every respect 在每一方面

40. untidy [ʌnˈtaɪdɪ] (adj.) 不整齊的
    【相關字彙】
    ³tidy [ˈtaɪdɪ] (adj.) 整潔的；整齊的

41. ⁴grave [grev] (adj.) ①重大的 ②莊重的；嚴肅的 (n.) 墓穴 (v.) 雕刻

42. ¹point ¹at (phr.) 指著
    【相關字彙與重要片語】
    ¹point [pɔɪnt] (v.) ①指向 ②指出 (n.) ①地點 ②得分 ③要點；中心思想 (phr.) ①in one's point of view 以……的觀點 ②come/get to the point 談到要點；直截了當地說 ③make a point of doing 特別注意做；重視做

43. ⁴tomb [tum] (n.) 墳墓；墓碑

44. carelessly [ˈkɛrlɪslɪ] (adv.) 不小心地；輕率地；草率地

45. disrespectfully [ˌdɪsrɪˈspɛktfəlɪ] (adv.) 不尊重地

46. ¹at ¹times (phr.) 有時；偶爾

47. ¹all ¹at ¹once（phr.）突然

48. ⁴arch［ɑrtʃ］（n.）①拱門 ②拱形

49. ¹for ¹a ¹while（phr.）暫時；一會兒

50. ²complete［kəm`plit］（adj.）①完全的 ②完整的 ③完成的
　　（v.）完成

51. ¹be dressed ¹in（phr.）穿著
　　【相關字彙】
　　dressed［drɛst］（adj.）穿好衣服的

52. ²wave［wev］（v.）①揮手 ②使成波形 　（n.）波浪；海浪
　　（phr.）make waves 興風作浪

53. ¹get ¹a ¹ride ¹from（phr.）讓某人搭車
　　【相關字彙與重要片語】
　　¹ride［raɪd］（v.）①搭乘 ②騎馬 　（n.）①乘坐 ②騎馬（或
　　乘車的）旅行 　（phr.）①ride out 安全渡過 ②take Sb. for
　　a ride 欺騙某人

54. ²therefore［`ðɛr.for］（adv.）因此
　　【諺】I think therefore I am. 我思故我在。

55. ¹in ⁶accordance ¹with（phr.）與……一致；依照
　　【相關字彙】
　　⁶accordance［ə`kɔrdns］（n.）一致

56. ¹agreement［ə`grimənt］（n.）①一致；同意 ②協定；契約
　　【相關字彙】
　　¹agree［ə`gri］（v.）同意；贊同

⁴agreeable [ə`griəbl]（adj.）①愉快的；宜人的 ②欣然贊同的

57. ²direction [də`rɛktʃən]（n.）①方向 ②指揮；指導 ③指示；說明

【相關字彙】

¹direct [də`rɛkt]（adj.）①直的（如道路）②直接的（adv.）直接地（v.）①指導 ②命令 ③指揮

²director [də`rɛktə]（n.）①指導者 ②（音樂）指揮；（電影）導演 ③董事

⁶directory [də`rɛktərɪ]（n.）①姓名住址簿；工商名錄；號碼簿 ②董事會；理事會

58. ³approach [ə`protʃ]（v.）①接近 ②即將達到（n.）①接近 ②方法；門徑（phr.）①approach Sb. on the matter 與某人商量此事 ②the approach of winter 冬天的臨近

59. ²however [hau`ɛvə]（conj.）然而；可是（adv.）無論如何

60. ¹after ¹a ¹while（phr.）過了一會兒；不久

61. ³float [flot]（v.）①漂浮 ②（貨幣）浮動（n.）漂浮物；浮標

62. ²passenger [`pæsndʒə]（n.）乘客；旅客

63. ¹next ¹to（phr.）①在……旁 ②接近；幾乎

64. ⁵shriek [ʃrik]（v.）/（n.）尖叫

65. ¹notice [`notɪs]（v.）注意（n.）①注意；察覺 ②警告 ③通知（phr.）①give notice 通知 ②at short notice 一接到通知（就……）③come into notice 引起注意

【相關字彙】

⁵noticeable [ˈnotɪsəbl̩] （adj.）顯著的；值得注意的

66. warning [ˈwɔrnɪŋ] （n.）警告；告誡

67. ¹be scared ¹to ¹death （phr.）嚇死了

【相關字彙】

scared [skɛrd] （adj.）吃驚的；害怕的

68. ¹step [stɛp] （v.）①步行 ②踩；踏 （n.）①腳步 ②台階
③步驟 （phr.）①step by step 一步一步地 ②mind/watch
your step 走路小心；言行小心謹慎 ③take steps 採取步驟
（或措施）

69. ¹gas [gæs] （n.）①氣體 ②瓦斯；汽油 ③（汽車的）油門

70. ⁶accelerate [ækˈsɛlərct] （v.）①使增速 ②促進；促使

71. ¹get ¹away ¹from （phr.）逃離

72. ²female [ˈfimel] （n.）/（adj.）女性（的）；雌性（的）

73. ³expectation [ˌɛkspɛkˈteʃən] （n.）期待；預期

【相關字彙】

²expect [ɪkˈspɛkt] （v.）預期；期待

74. eyeball [ˈaɪˌbɔl] （n.）眼球

75. ¹chase [tʃes] （v.）①追趕 ②驅逐 （n.）①追逐 ②打獵
（phr.）①in chase of 追逐 ②chase after rainbows 想入非非
☆ ¹rainbow （n.）彩虹

76. ²sign [saɪn] （n.）①記號；符號 ②手勢；姿勢 ③徵兆
（v.）簽名 （phr.）①sign language 手語 ②sign in/out 簽

到/退 ③make/give a sign to 向……做暗號

【相關字彙】

⁴signature [ˈsɪɡnətʃɚ] （n.）簽名；署名

77. ⁵despair [dɪˈspɛr]（n.）/（v.）絕望；失望

78. ³faint [fent]（adj.）微弱的；模糊的　（v.）昏厥

79. ³trace [tres]（v.）①描繪 ②追蹤；追溯　（n.）①蹤跡 ②痕跡 ③絲毫；少許

80. ¹light [laɪt]（n.）①光；光線；光亮 ②電燈　（v.）①點火；點燃 ②照亮 ③使容光煥發　（adj.）①明亮的 ②淺色的 ③輕的　（phr.）①light bulb 燈泡 ②light up 照亮；點燃；使容光煥發 ③make light of 輕視

【相關字彙】

³lighthouse [ˈlaɪtˌhaʊs]（n.）燈塔

81. ²path [pæθ]（n.）①小路；小徑 ②途徑；軌道　（phr.）stand in Sb.'s path 阻礙某人如願

82. surprisingly [səˈpraɪzɪŋlɪ]（adv.）驚訝地

【相關字彙與重要片語】

¹surprise [səˈpraɪz]（n.）①驚奇 ②驚人的事物　（v.）使驚奇　（phr.）be surprised at/by 對……感到驚奇

83. ¹be ³surrounded ¹by（phr.）被……包圍

【相關字彙】

³surround [səˈraʊnd]（v.）包圍；環繞

⁴surroundings [səˈraʊndɪŋz]（n.）環境

84. ¹run ¹out ¹of（phr.）①用完 ②自……跑出

85. ¹in ¹a ²hurry（phr.）匆忙地

　　【相關字彙與重要片語】

　　²hurry［`hɝɪ］（n.）匆促；急忙 （v.）①催促 ②趕緊；匆忙（phr.）hurry Sb. into doing 催某人立即做某事

86. awkwardly［`ɔkwɝdlɪ］（adv.）笨拙地；不靈巧地

　　【相關字彙】

　　⁴awkward［`ɔkwəd］（adj.）笨拙的；不靈巧的

87. ³balance［`bæləns］（v.）①保持平衡 ②結算（帳戶）（n.）①平衡；均衡 ②結存；結餘 （phr.）①balanced diet 均衡飲食 ②keep/lose one's balance 保持/失去 平衡 ③be/hang in the balance 懸而未決 ☆ ³diet（n.）飲食

88. ⁴flee［fli］（v.）逃離；逃走

89. ⁵enthusiastic［ɪnˌθjuzɪ`æstɪk］（adj.）狂熱的；熱心的（phr.）be enthusiastic about/over/at 對……熱心的

　　【相關字彙】

　　⁴enthusiasm［ɪn`θjuzɪˌæzəm］（n.）狂熱；熱心

90. ¹pay ²attention ¹to（phr.）注意

　　【相關字彙與重要片語】

　　²attention［ə`tɛnʃən］（n.）①注意；專心 ②照顧；治療（phr.）draw attention 引起注意

　　☆ ¹draw（v.）吸引；招來

91. ¹a ¹lot ¹of（phr.）很多的

92. ¹try one's ¹best（phr.）盡全力；盡最大努力

93. ²explain [ɪkˋsplen]（v.）說明；解釋　（phr.）explain oneself 把自己的意思解釋清楚（或解釋自己的行為）

94. ²realize [ˋrɪəˌlaɪz]（v.）①了解；領悟 ②實現

95. frightful [ˋfraɪtfəl]（adj.）恐怖的

    【相關字彙】

    ²fright [fraɪt]（n.）驚懼；恐怖

96. ²hang [hæŋ]（v.）①懸；掛 ②吊死；絞死　（n.）（口）做法；訣竅　（phr.）①hang on 握住不放；堅持下去；（打電話時）不掛斷 ②hang up 掛斷電話 ③get the hang of 懂得訣竅

97. ³shadow [ˋʃædo]（n.）①影子 ②映象 ③蔭；幽暗處（phr.）①catch at shadows 捕風捉影；白費力氣 ②be afraid of one's own shadow 非常膽怯

98. ¹prove [pruv]（v.）①證明；證實 ②檢驗　（phr.）prove out 成功；如所預期

    【相關字彙與重要片語】

    ³proof [pruf]（n.）①證據；物證 ②證明；證實 ③檢驗（phr.）①give proof of 證明 ②in proof of 當……的證據 ③make proof of 提出證據

99. ³existence [ɪgˋzɪstəns]（n.）①存在 ②生存

    【相關字彙】

    ²exist [ɪgˋzɪst]（v.）①存在；實有 ②生存；活著

~ 第四章 ~
# 我的女朋友

有一個可怕的故事報導，關於在許多年前，英格蘭（England），伯明罕（Bermingham），的一對青少年男女朋友，伊帆與小藝。這男孩非常地喜歡他的女朋友。他們之間有一種特殊的激情（[4]chemistry）存在著。小藝是一位很有魅力的（charming）女孩，她有一百（[1]hundred）六十八公分（[3]centimeter）高。她是一位金髮美人。伊帆對她感到非常地驕傲，並且經常對人們誇耀（[4]boast）著，他擁有一位幾乎沒有任何缺點（[6]defect）完美的（[2]perfect）女朋友。

但是，男孩對他女朋友的愛是如此地激烈的（[1]strong），以至於他忍不住想要控制（[2]control）住她。有一天，他突然地

∾ Chapter 4 ∾
My Girlfriend

There was a scary story reported about [1]a pair of teens who were boyfriend and girlfriend, Evan and Little Art, in [2]Birmingham, [3]England many years ago. The boy liked his girlfriend very much. There was [4]a kind of special [5]chemistry existing between them. Little Art was a very [6]charming girl who was one [7]hundred and sixty-eight-[8]centimeters tall. She was a [9]blonde bombshell. Evan was very [10]proud of her, and he often [11]boasted to people that he had a [12]perfect girlfriend with almost no [13]defects.

But the love of the boy for his girlfriend was so [14]strong that he [15]could not but [16]control her. One day, an [17]odd idea （abruptly）想起了一個怪異的（³odd）念頭。他能夠藉由在她身上惡作劇來報復他的女朋友。但是，為什麼他想要去報復（⁶retaliate）呢？他想要報復主要的原因（¹reason）是這樣的：他的女朋友幾乎是完美的與美好的人，除了她所擁有的一個習慣（²habit）之外。不久，伊帆受夠了這個習慣，而他無法能再忍受（⁴endure）這個習慣下去了。

然後，事情轉變（¹turn）成甚至是更糟糕的（¹worse）了。這對情侶在無數次的（⁴numerous）、沒有效率的（ineffective）溝通（⁴communication）關於（⁴regarding）小藝的習慣之後，雖然（²although）普通的（³normal）吵架（³quarrel），或者，甚至是更嚴重的爭吵（¹fight）持續上演著，這女孩依然無法對她的習慣做出任何的改變。那麼，是什麼習慣讓她的男朋友感到十分地不悅呢？

[18]came to him [19]abruptly. He could [20]take revenge on his girlfriend by [21]playing a trick on her. But why did he want to [22]retaliate? The main [23]reason for him wanting revenge was this: his girlfriend was almost perfect and was a wonderful person [24]except for one habit she had. After a while, Evan was [25]fed up with the [26]habit, and he could [27]not [28]endure it anymore.

Then things [29]turned even [30]worse. After the lovers' [31]numerous times of [32]ineffective [33]communication [34]regarding Little Art's habit, [35]although many [36]normal [37]quarrels, or even more serious [38]fights kept happening, the girl was still [39]unable to [40]make any changes to her habit. So, what was the habit which made her boyfriend feel so bad?

　　原來（orginally），小藝是一位在性格上帶有很獨特的（⁴peculiar），或者是神祕的特質（²quality）的女孩。她習慣性地只喜歡她自己一個人散步到一座森林裡去。實際上，沒有人真正地知道，為何她偶爾需要到森林之中。所以，為何她要去呢？由於她短暫的（³temporary）消失（disappearance），讓伊帆一點兒也看不到、找不到她。她變成了在世界上的一名失蹤人口。這將使得他變得生氣、發瘋。男孩也無法忍受他的女朋友頻繁增加地（increasingly）消失不見。她甚至是從不留下一張便條（¹note）給他。伊帆想要他的女朋友更多的陪伴（²company），因為，他是一位有控制慾望類型（²type）的人（²guy）。

　　在那一刻，伊帆心裡想著他將只是小小地惡作劇一番，想著這個惡作劇將是不會傷害（¹hurt）任何人的吧！」他打扮自己像是一隻大猩猩（⁵gorilla）。他穿上黑色的裝束（⁴costume），並且戴著可怕的頭飾（headgear）。然後，他站

^{41}Originally, Little Art was a girl who had a very ^{42}peculiar or mysterious ^{43}quality in her personality. She sometimes liked to walk to a forest only ^{44}by herself. Actually, there was no one who really knew why she needed to go to the forest ^{45}once in a while. So why did she go? Evan could not see or find her at all because of her ^{46}temporary ^{47}disappearances. She became ^{48}a missing person to the world. This made him get angry and ^{49}go crazy. The boy also could not ^{50}put up with his girlfriend's ^{51}increasingly frequent disappearances. She never even left a ^{52}note for him. Evan wanted more ^{53}company from his girlfriend because he was a controlling ^{54}type of ^{55}guy.

At that point, Evan thought that he would ^{56}pull just a small prank, thinking it wouldn't ^{57}hurt anybody. He dressed himself as a ^{58}gorilla. He ^{59}put on a black ^{60}costume and wore a scary ^{61}headgear. Then, he stood at the place where they had

在他們先前（previously）承諾（²promise）彼此碰面的地方，一些樹旁邊的一條十字路口（⁶intersection）上。而他，則躲在那些樹的後面等待著女主角（protagonist）的到來。

　　不久後，他的女朋友小藝，按照約定的時間前來。同一時間，當她出現（¹appear）時穿著紅上衣（³blouse）與紅靴（³boot），伊帆突然從一顆大樹後面往前一跳（¹jump）出來，跳到小藝的面前嚇壞了她。果然，他粗魯地（brusquely）把小藝弄哭了。男孩一看到他成功（²succeed）了，他就對此惡作劇感到後悔了。他心想這一次是做得太過分了。

　　所以，他脫下頭套並停止（⁴cease）了他的惡作劇，而且笨拙地（clumsily）試著安慰（³comfort）著他的女朋友，告訴她不要哭。他向她道歉著，並懇求她的原諒，說著他不應該愚

[62]promised to meet each other [63]previously at an [64]intersection next to some trees. And he hid behind those trees and [65]waited for the female [66]protagonist to come.

[67]Soon after, his girlfriend Little Art came in accordance with the agreed time. [68]At the same time, when she [69]appeared in the red [70]blouse and [71]boots, Evan suddenly [72]jumped out, in front of the girl, to scare her from behind a big tree. [73]Sure enough, he [74]brusquely made her cry. As soon as the boy saw that he [75]succeeded, he was [76]regretful about the trick. He thought he had [77]gone too far this time.

So, he [78]took off the headgear and [79]ceased his trick. And he also [80]clumsily tried to [81]comfort his girlfriend, telling her not to cry. He [82]apologized to her and [83]prayed for her forgiveness,

弄她。他一直是非常輕地（gently）撫摸（⁶caress）著她的手。她漸漸地（gradually）停止住了哭泣而心情（³mood）再一次變得平靜（²calm）下來。最後，她甚至咯咯地笑（⁶chuckle）了起來，而說她不再會責備（⁵condemn）她的男朋友了。但是，接下來，女孩竟然剝去了她的臉皮，彷彿容易地脫掉（³remove）了面具（²mask）一般。結果，她七孔流血，並對著他露出一張非常猙獰的（⁵grim）、可怕的臉。

saying he should not have tricked her. He kept [84]caressing her hands very [85]gently. She [86]gradually stopped crying, and her [87]mood became [88]calm again. Finally, she even [89]chuckled and said she did not [90]condemn her boyfriend anymore. But then, the girl [91]peeled the skin off her face as if easily [92]removing a [93]mask. [94]As a result, her [95]seven holes bled, and she showed a very [96]grim and scary face to him.

Chapter 4

Vocabulary

1. ¹a ¹pair ¹of（phr.）一雙；一對

2. Bermingham [ˋbɝmɪŋˌhæm] 伯明罕市（英國城市名）

3. England [ˋɪŋɡlənd] 英國；英格蘭

4. ¹a ¹kind ¹of（phr.）一種
   【相關字彙】
   ¹kind [kaɪnd]（adj.）親切的；和善的　（n.）種類

5. ⁴chemistry [ˋkɛmɪstrɪ]（n.）①化學　②（男女間的）激情；
   來電
   【相關字彙】
   ²chemical [ˋkɛmɪkl]（adj.）化學的；化學上的
   ⁵chemist [ˋkɛmɪst]（n.）化學家

6. charming [ˋtʃɑrmɪŋ]（adj.）迷人的
   【相關字彙與重要片語】
   ³charm [tʃɑrm]（n.）①魅力　②符咒；咒語　（v.）①誘惑；
   使陶醉　②施行魔法　（phr.）①under the charm 著迷　②be
   charmed with 給……迷住

7. ¹hundred [ˋhʌndrəd]（n.）/（adj.）百（的）　（phr.）hundreds
   of 數百的

8. ³centimeter [ˋsɛntəˌmitɚ]（n.）公分

9. ⁵blonde bombshell（phr.）金髮碧眼的美女

【相關字彙】

⁵blond/⁵blonde [blɑnd]（adj.）金髮的；（皮膚）白皙的（n.）金髮膚白碧眼的人

bombshell [ˈbɑmˌʃɛl]（n.）①炸彈 ②驚人的事（或話）③（俗）美女

10. ¹be ²proud ¹of（phr.）驕傲

【相關字彙與重要片語】

²proud [praʊd]（adj.）①驕傲的 ②自豪的；得意的

【諺】Knowledge makes one humble；ignorance makes one proud. 知識使人謙遜，而無知則使人傲慢。

²knowledge（n.）知識　²humble（adj.）謙虛的

³ignorance（n.）無知

²pride [praɪd]（v.）使自負；驕傲　（n.）①自豪；得意 ②驕傲；傲慢 ③引以自豪的人（或物）　（phr.）①peacock in his pride 開屏的孔雀 ②pride oneself on 以……自豪 ③take（a）pride in 以……自豪 ☆ ⁵peacock（n.）孔雀

【諺】Pride goes before a fall. 驕者必敗。

11. ⁴boast [bost]（v.）自誇；自大　（n.）自負（的事）

12. ²perfect [ˈpɝfɪkt]（adj.）①完美的 ②完全的 ③精通的　（v.）使完美　（phr.）perfect oneself in 嫻熟；精通

13. ⁶defect [dɪˈfɛkt]（n.）缺點；短處；缺陷

14. ¹strong [strɔŋ]（adj.）①（感情等）激烈的 ②強大的 ③堅

固的

15. cannot ¹but V.（phr.）不得不

16. ²control [kən`trol]（n.）/（v.）控制；支配；抑制 （phr.）
①birth control 節育 ②control oneself 自制 ③take control of
掌管

17. ³odd [ɑd]（adj.）①奇怪的；怪異的 ②（數）奇數的；單
數的

18. ¹come ¹to（phr.）突然想起

19. abruptly [ə`brʌptlɪ]（adv.）①突然地 ②（態度上）唐突地
③陡峭地
【相關字彙】
⁵abrupt [ə`brʌpt]（adj.）①突然的 ②（態度上）唐突的 ③
陡峭的

20. ¹take ⁴revenge ¹on（phr.）報復
【相關字彙】
⁴revenge [rɪ`vɛndʒ]（n.）/（v.）復仇；報復
【諺】Pardon is the most glorious revenge.
寬恕是最好的報復。
²pardon（v.）原諒 ⁴glorious（adj.）榮耀的

21. ¹play ¹a ²trick ¹on Sb.（phr.）對某人惡作劇
【相關字彙與重要片語】
²trick [trɪk]（n.）①詭計；騙局 ②惡作劇；開玩笑 ③把戲
（v.）欺騙（phr.）①a dirty/mean trick 卑鄙手段 ②get/

learn the trick of it 學會訣竅 ③trick Sb. into doing St. 哄騙某人做事情 ☆ ¹dirty/¹mean（adj.）卑鄙的

【諺】You cannot teach an old dog new <u>tricks</u>.

老狗學不了新把戲。

22. ⁶retaliate [rɪˋtælɪˏet]（v.）報復

23. ¹reason [ˋrizn]（n.）①<u>理由；動機</u> ②理性 ③道理 （v.）推論；推理 （phr.）①lose one's reason 喪失理智 ②reason with 勸導 ③reason out（根據推理）想出

24. ¹except ¹for（phr.）除了……以外

【相關字彙】

¹except/¹excepting [ɪkˋsɛpt]／[ɪkˋsɛptɪŋ]（v.）除去；除外（prep.）除了……之外

⁴exception [ɪkˋsɛpʃən]（n.）例外

⁵exceptional [ɪkˋsɛpʃən!]（adj.）例外的；特殊的

25. ¹be ¹fed ¹up ¹with（phr.）受夠了

【相關字彙】

¹feed [fid]（v.）餵（養）；飼（養）

26. ²habit [ˋhæbɪt]（n.）習慣；習性 （phr.）be in/have the/a habit of doing 有做……的習慣

27. ¹not…anymore（phr.）不再

28. ⁴endure [ɪnˋdjʊr]（v.）忍耐；忍受

【相關字彙】

⁶endurance [ɪnˋdjʊrəns]（n.）忍耐

29. [1]turn [tɜn] （v.）①轉身 ②變得；成為 ③翻轉；轉動 （n.）①轉動 ②轉彎 ③轉變 （phr.）①turn down 拒絕 ②turn out 結果是；證明是 ③turn against 敵視；反對 【諺】Even a worm will <u>turn</u>. 狗急跳牆。 [1]worm（n.）蟲

30. [1]worse [wɜs]（adj.）/（adv.）更糟

31. [4]numerous [ˋnjumərəs]（adj.）無數的；很多的

32. ineffective [ɪnəˋfɛktɪv]（adj.）無效的
    【相關字彙與重要片語】
    [2]effective [ɪˋfɛktɪv]（adj.）①有效的 ②生效的
    [2]effect [ɪˋfɛkt]（n.）①結果 ②影響；效果 （phr.）①cause and effect 有因果關係的 ②come/go into effect 生效

33. [4]communication [kəˋmjunəˏkeʃən]（n.）①傳達；傳遞 ②<u>溝通；交流</u>
    【相關字彙】
    [3]communicate [kəˋmjunəˏket]（v.）交流；溝通
    [6]communicative [kəˋmjunəˏketɪv]（adj.）①愛說話的；暢談的；愛社交的 ②交際的

34. [4]regarding [rɪˋgɑrdɪŋ]（prep.）關於
    【相關字彙與重要片語】
    [2]regard [rɪˋgɑrd]（v.）①認為 ②注意 ③尊重 （n.）①注意；關心 ②尊重 ③考慮 （phr.）①regard as 把……視為 ②without regard to 不考慮 ③in/with regard to 關於

35. [2]although [ɔlˋðo]（conj.）雖然；即使

【相關字彙】

¹though〔ðo〕（conj.）雖然；即使

36. ³normal〔ˈnɔrml〕（adj.）正常的；標準的；普通的

【相關字彙】

⁶norm〔nɔrm〕（n.）基準；規範

37. ³quarrel〔ˈkwɔrəl〕（n.）/（v.）<u>口角；爭吵</u>（phr.）quarrel with 和……爭吵；不同意

【諺】It takes two to make a <u>quarrel</u>. 一個巴掌拍不響。

【相關字彙】

⁶quarrelsome〔ˈkwɔrəlsəm〕（adj.）愛爭吵的

38. ¹fight〔faɪt〕（v.）/（n.）①打仗；戰鬥 ②<u>爭吵</u>（phr.）①fight against 抵抗 ②fight it out 鬥爭到底

【相關字彙】

²fighter〔ˈfaɪtɚ〕（n.）戰士；戰鬥者

39. ¹be unable ¹to V.（phr.）無法做

40. ¹make（¹a）²change（s）¹to（phr.）對……做改變

【相關字彙與重要片語】

²change〔tʃendʒ〕（v.）①變化；改變 ②換乘（車等）（n.）①變化；變更；變遷 ②零錢（phr.）change of heart 變心

【諺】The leopard cannot <u>change</u> his spots.

江山易改，本性難移。 ²leopard（n.）豹

²spot（n.）斑點

41. orginally [əˋrɪdʒənḷɪ]（adv.）起初；原來

42. ⁴peculiar [pɪˋkjuljə]（adj.）①<u>獨特的</u> ②奇怪的

43. ²quality [ˋkwɑlətɪ]（n.）①品質 ②<u>特質；特性</u>

44. ¹by oneself（phr.）獨自

45. ¹once ¹in ¹a ¹while（phr.）偶爾

46. ³temporary [ˋtɛmpəˏrɛrɪ]（adj.）暫時的；臨時的

47. disappearance [ˏdɪsəˋpɪrəns]（n.）消失

【相關字彙】

²disappear [ˏdɪsəˋpɪr]（v.）消失不見

48. ¹a ³missing ¹person（phr.）失蹤人口

【相關字彙】

³missing [ˋmɪsɪŋ]（adj.）①行蹤不明的 ②缺掉的

49. ¹go ²crazy（phr.）發瘋

50. ¹put ¹up ¹with（phr.）忍受

51. increasingly [ɪnˋkrisɪŋli]（adv.）增加地

【相關字彙】

²increase [ɪnˋkris]（v.）／（n.）增加

52. ¹note [not]（n.）①筆記；記錄 ②注意 ③<u>便條</u>（v.）①注意 ②記下；記錄 ③對……加註釋 （phr.）①make/take notes 做筆記 ②take note of 注意

53. ²company [ˋkʌmpənɪ]（n.）①朋友；同伴 ②公司 ③<u>陪伴</u>（phr.）keep company with 與……在一起
【諺】Misery loves <u>company</u>. 禍不單行。³misery（n.）不幸

54. ^{2}type [taɪp]（n.）①典型 ②類型 ③字體 （v.）打字

【相關字彙】

^{3}typewriter [ˈtaɪpˌraɪtə]（n.）打字機

55. ^{2}guy [gaɪ]（n.）（口）傢伙；人

56. ^{1}pull ^{1}a prank（n.）惡作劇

【相關字彙】

prank [præŋk]（n.）/（v.） 惡作劇

57. ^{1}hurt [hɝt]（v.）①使傷害 ②損害 ③使疼痛 （n.）傷；痛

58. ^{5}gorilla [gəˈrɪlə]（n.）大猩猩

59. ^{1}put ^{1}on（phr.）穿上

60. ^{4}costume [ˈkʌstjum]（n.）服裝；裝束

61. headgear [ˈhɛdˌgɪr]（n.）頭套；頭飾

62. ^{2}promise [ˈprɑmɪs]（n.）①諾言；約定 ②希望；前途 （v.）答應；允諾 （phr.）①keep one's promise 遵守諾言 ②break a/one's promise 不守諾言；食言 ③A promise is a promise. 諾言就是諾言（不得違背）

【相關字彙】

^{4}promising [ˈprɑmɪsɪŋ]（adj.）有前途的；有希望的

63. previously [ˈpriviəslɪ]（adv.）以前地；先前地

【相關字彙】

^{3}previous [ˈpriviəs]（adj.）以前的；先前的

64. ^{6}intersection [ˌɪntəˈsɛkʃən]（n.）①橫斷；交叉 ②（道路）十字路口

65. ¹wait ¹for（phr.）等待

【諺】Time and tide <u>wait for</u> no man. 歲月不待人。

³tide（n.）潮汐

66. protagonist [proˋtægənɪst]（n.）主角

67. ¹soon ¹after（phr.）不久之後

68. ¹at ¹the ¹same ¹time（phr.）同時

69. ¹appear [əˋpɪr]（v.）①<u>出現</u> ②似乎；看來好像

70. ³blouse [blaʊs]（n.）（女用）短上衣；短襯衫

71. ³boot [but]（n.）長（筒）靴

72. ¹jump [dʒʌmp]（v.）/（n.）跳躍

73. ¹sure ¹enough（phr.）果真

【相關字彙與重要片語】

¹sure [ʃʊr]（adj.）①確信的 ②確實的 ③一定的 （phr.）①for sure 確實；一定會 ②sure thing 必然之事；一定成功的事 ③be/feel sure of oneself 有自信

74. brusquely [ˋbrʌsklɪ]（adv.）粗魯地；粗率地

75. ²succeed [səkˋsid]（v.）①<u>成功</u> ②繼承；繼任 （phr.）①succeed in 成功；順利完成 ②succeed to 繼承；繼任

【相關字彙與重要片語】

²success [səkˋsɛs]（n.）①成功 ②成功的人（或事物）（phr.）make a success of 把……做得很成功

76. ¹be regretful ¹about（phr.）後悔

【相關字彙】

³regret〔rɪˋgrɛt〕（v.）／（n.）①後悔；遺憾 ②悲痛；哀悼

77. ¹go ¹too ¹far（phr.）做事情太過分

78. ¹take ¹off（phr.）脫下

79. ⁴cease〔sis〕（v.）停止；終止

80. clumsily〔ˋklʌmzɪlɪ〕（adv.）笨拙地

　　【相關字彙】

　　⁴clumsy〔ˋklʌmzɪ〕（adj.）笨拙的；不靈活的

81. ³comfort〔ˋkʌmfət〕（n.）①安慰 ②舒適；安逸 （v.）<u>安慰</u>

82. ⁴apologize ¹to（phr.）道歉

　　【相關字彙】

　　⁴apologize〔əˋpɑlədʒaɪz〕（v.）道歉；謝罪

　　⁴apology〔əˋpɑlədʒɪ〕（n.）道歉，賠罪

83. ²pray ¹for（phr.）祈禱

　　【相關字彙】

　　²pray〔pre〕（v.）①祈禱 ②請求；懇求

　　³prayer〔prɛr〕（n.）祈禱；祈禱文

84. ⁶caress〔kəˋrɛs〕（v.）／（n.）愛撫

85. gently〔ˋdʒɛntlɪ〕（adv.）輕輕地；柔和地

　　【相關字彙】

　　²gentle〔ˋdʒɛntl̩〕（adj.）①和善的；溫和的 ②和緩的；輕柔的 ③馴服的

86. gradually〔ˋgrædʒʊəlɪ〕（adv.）逐漸地

　　【相關字彙】

^{3}gradual [ˈɡrædʒʊəl]（adj.）逐漸的

87. ^{3}mood [mud]（n.）情緒；心情 （phr.）in the/a mood for/ to do 有/做 ……的興致

88. ^{2}calm [kɑm]（adj.）/（v.）/（n.）平靜；冷靜 （phr.） calm down 冷靜

【諺】After a storm comes a calm. 雨過天晴；否極泰來。

89. ^{6}chuckle [ˈtʃʌkl]（v.）咯咯笑

90. ^{5}condemn [kənˈdɛm]（v.）①譴責；責備 ②宣告有罪；判刑

91. ^{3}peel ^{1}off（phr.）去掉；脫掉
【相關字彙】
^{3}peel [pil]（v.）剝皮；削皮；去皮

92. ^{3}remove [rɪˈmuv]（v.）①移動 ②脫掉；除去 ③免職

93. ^{2}mask [mæsk]（n.）①面具 ②口罩 （phr.）①assume/put on/wear a mask 戴假面具；隱藏真相 ②throw off one's mask 摘下假面具；現出原來面目
☆ ^{4}assume（v.）假裝 ^{1}throw ^{1}off（phr.）扔掉

94. ^{1}as ^{1}a ^{2}result（phr.）結果
【相關字彙】
^{2}result [rɪˈzʌlt]（n.）結果 （v.）①由……發生 ②導致

95. ^{1}seven ^{1}holes ^{3}bleed（phr.）七孔流血
【相關字彙與重要片語】
^{1}hole [hol]（n.）洞；孔；破洞 （phr.）make a hole in 大量耗費

³bleed ［blid］（v.）流血

96. ⁵grim ［grɪm］（adj.）陰森的；猙獰的

～ 第五章 ～
十三號病房

在馬尼拉（Manila），菲律賓（Philippines），一九九〇年代，一名年輕業餘的（⁴amateur）給取名（¹name）修平的音樂家（²musician），受癌症（²cancer）之苦，而身處於極度的痛苦之中。甚至，由於癌細胞（²cell）在他的身上擴散（proliferation）著，病情變得更加地嚴重。他於是從診所（³clinic），馬上被轉移（⁴transfer）至一間較大型的、附近的醫院去接受（¹receive）更專業的（⁴professional）治療。急救過後，他被安置在一間雙人的加護病房（⁵ward）裡。他剛好搬進去的病房號碼爲十三號。現在的他，必須躺（¹lie）在床上休息來恢復（³recover）健康（¹health）。

過了許久之後，修平醒了。他環顧著住的病房四處。

⌒ Chapter 5 ⌒
The 13th Ward

In [1]Manila, [2]Philippines, in the 1990s, an [3]amateur young
[4]musician, [5]named Xiu-ping, who suffered from [6]cancer and
stayed [7]in agony, became even sicker because of the [8]proliferation
of the cancer [9]cells in his body. He was then [10]transferred from a
[11]clinic to a larger hospital nearby to [12]receive more [13]professional
treatment immediately. After some [14]first aid, he was [15]placed in
a two-person [16]intensive care unit. The number of the [17]ward
he just [18]moved into was thirteen. Now he needed to [19]lie in
bed to [20]recover his [21]health.

After a very long time, Xiu-ping woke up. He [22]looked

他發現到病房右邊另一位病人（²patient）的病床，明顯地（obviously）被一塊白色帷幔（²drape）圍住，而完全地遮掩著病床。幾位護士說，她是一位即將往生年老的女士。那天早上，醫生們對於她的診斷（⁶diagnosis）做了一份很正式的（²formal）報告，並且宣佈（³announce）這名老婦人或許（³might）今晚是無法活著渡過難關了。老婦人的先生是一位年長的紳士（²gentleman），他前來見這名老婦人，他親愛的太太，最後一次面。在稍早醫生們講（²deliver）了這壞消息（¹news）之後，他在下午三點鐘時就去與她訣別了。

在用過了一些清湯（⁵broth）當作晚餐後，這位年輕病人睡著了。夜間（nighttime）的時候，因癌症所造成許多身體的（⁴physical）疼痛（²pain），修平一直睡得不是很好和安穩地（smoothly）。當他半睡半醒之間，他覺得好像在這間小病房內，有個幻影不斷地（constantly）來來回回地移動著。他對

around the room where he lived. He found that the other [23]patient's bed on the right side of the ward was [24]obviously surrounded by a white [25]drape to [26]cover it up completely. Several nurses said that she was an old lady who was [27]about to die. That morning, the doctors made a [28]formal report of her [29]diagnoses and [30]announced that the old woman [31]might not [32]make it through tonight. The old woman's husband, an elderly [33]gentleman, came to see this old lady, his dear wife, [34]for the last time. He went to say goodbye to her at three o'clock in the afternoon after the doctors [35]delivered the bad [36]news earlier.

After having some [37]broth for dinner, the young patient [38]fell asleep. During the [39]nighttime, because of the many [40]physical [41]pains [42]resulting from cancer, Xiu-ping did not sleep very well nor [43]smoothly. As he was [44]lying half awake, he felt as if there was a shadow [45]constantly moving [46]back and forth within the

此感到疑惑（²wonder）：「這病房會有竊賊（³burglar）闖入嗎？」但是，關於這件事他實在是毫無頭緒哩！

　　接著，他有點試著調整（⁴adjust）著他的呼吸，使得呼吸變得更為順暢。突然，修平聽到了正來自他隔壁，另一位病人的床，一些怪異好似活動的聲音。他也聽到某人咳嗽（²cough）與吃東西的聲音。這名年輕男子無法抵抗（³resist）心中強烈的好奇心（⁴curiosity），所以，他安靜地舉起（¹lift）靠近他白色帷幔（²curtain）的一角（²corner），而從右手邊看著另一病人的床。但是，他沒注意到任何事物，除了一位老夫人寂靜地（silently）、不動地（motionlessly）躺在病床上外。她正依賴著呼吸器（respirator）維持著，她虛弱的（¹weak）、脆弱（⁶fragile）不堪的生命。

little ward. "Is there a [47]burglar [48]breaking into this ward?" he [49]wondered. But he really [50]did not have a clue about it!

Then, he tried to [51]adjust his breathing a bit to make it smoother. Suddenly, Xiu-ping heard some weird sounds like movements [52]coming from the other patient's bed next to him. He also heard a few sounds of someone's [53]coughing and eating, too. The young man could not [54]resist his strong [55]curiosity, so he quietly [56]lifted one [57]corner of the white [58]curtain near him and looked, from his right side, at the other patient's bed. But he did not notice anything except that an old lady was lying in bed [59]silently and [60]motionlessly. She was [61]relying on a [62]respirator to maintain her [63]weak and [64]fragile life.

　　很快地，由於藥物（²drug）的副作用的關係，年輕人
再次想睡了。他所服用藥物劇烈地（drastically）起了作用
（²function）。同時，他感覺到如此多的寒意更靠近著他，而
且甚至有陣陣冰冷的（freezing）風，強烈地襲擊（¹hit）到他
的身上來。睡覺時，他故意（intentionally）保持他的眼睛部分
地（partially）張開著，而驚訝地，老婦人不但依然還是活著的
（²alive），且就正站在他的床前。

　　年輕人感到十分地害怕，並且，無法理解（¹understand）
爲什麼老婦人詭異地出現在他的床邊。老婦人的面容
（⁶complexion）是黑色的；但是，她看起來對他來說有一
些和藹可親的（⁶amiable）樣子。她以一種很低沉、嘶啞的
（⁵hoarse）聲音（¹voice）對他說著話：「喂！年輕人！目前據
我所知，你還是十分地年輕；但是你卻有一個可能無法治癒
的（incurable）疾病（³disease）。假定（³suppose）我能幫助你
從癌症中康復起來，你是否願意付（¹pay）出任何代價，來交

Soon, the young man ⁶⁵felt sleepy again because of the ⁶⁶side effects of the ⁶⁷drugs. The drugs he had taken ⁶⁸functioned ⁶⁹drastically. At the same time, he felt so much coldness coming closer to him, and even ⁷⁰gusts of ⁷¹freezing wind ⁷²hit him hard. He ⁷³intentionally kept his eyes ⁷⁴partially open while sleeping, and surprisingly, the old lady was not only still ⁷⁵alive, but was standing at the front of his bed.

Xiu-ping felt very afraid and could not ⁷⁶understand why the old woman strangely appeared at his bedside. The old lady had a dark ⁷⁷complexion, but she looked a bit ⁷⁸amiable to him. She spoke to him in a very low and ⁷⁹hoarse ⁸⁰voice: "Hey, young man, ⁸¹as far as I know, you are still very young, but you possibly have an ⁸²incurable ⁸³disease. ⁸⁴Suppose that I can help you ⁸⁵recover from your cancer, are you willing to ⁸⁶pay anything ⁸⁷in exchange for your life? ⁸⁸Of course, under these

換你生命呢？當然，在這些條件（³condition）之下是不會傷害（³harm）任何其他人的。」

　　當他注意聽著女士所對他所說了的話，這名男子實際上猶豫（³hesitate）著：「她是如何知道任何有關我疾病的事情呢？也許她說的是事實。還有什麼是像她所提起的，在世界上，有比身體健康更重要的（¹important）其它任何事情了呢？除此之外，老婆婆說了這件事將並不會傷害到其他任何人啊！那是真的嗎？」他深思熟慮（⁶deliberate）了好一會兒（⁵awhile）；最後卻是答應（⁵consent）了。那就是他為自己做了一項重要的決定。他下定決心去順從，不論什麼（²whatever），這位年老的女士對他所建議（³suggest）的事。在他與老婦人達成了協議之後，沒一會兒，年輕人便沉睡了過去。

[89]conditions, it will not [90]harm any other persons."

The man actually [91]hesitated when he [92]listened to what the lady had said: "How does she know anything about my illness? Maybe she is telling the truth. Is there anything else more [93]important than physical health in the world as she [94]brought up? [95]In addition, the old lady said that it would not harm any other people! Is that true?" He [96]deliberated [97]awhile but finally [98]consented. [99]That is, he [100]made an important decision for himself. He [101]made up his mind to follow [102]whatever the old lady [103]suggested to him. After he [104]reached an agreement with the old woman, [105]in an instant, the young man [106]fell into a deep sleep.

　　隔天一早，一些醫療人員進到病房內。他們發現了老婆婆往生了，她很有可能昨晚過世的。他們卻不知她死亡確切的（²exact）時間。在她旁邊的心電圖（electrocardiogram），其上已無顯示任何心跳（heartbeat）的跡象。然而，當一名護士推著修平坐在輪椅（⁵wheelchair）上去複診時，他的醫生奇蹟地（miraculously）察覺到，一個有關年輕人病況的事實：在他身體內的癌細胞已憑空消失了！當醫生與護士正準備通知這名年輕人此好消息時；他們卻驚懼（⁴horrify）聽到了年輕人的聲音。他聽起來就如同已死去的（deceased）婦人的聲音那般。他無意地（casually）詢問他們一個問題（¹question）：「我的老伴呢？今天是我們結婚第四十（fortieth）年的結婚紀念日啊！」

The next morning, some medical workers came into the ward. They found the old lady dead; she had probably died last night. But they did not know the [107]exact time of her death. There wasn't any sign of a [108]heartbeat showing on the [109]electrocardiogram beside her already. However, when a nurse pushed Xiu-ping in his [110]wheelchair to have a [111]subsequent consultation, his doctor [112]miraculously discovered the truth about the young patient's condition: the cancer cells in his body had disappeared [113]into thin air! While the doctor and nurse were preparing to [114]inform the young man of the good news, they were [115]horrified to hear the young man's voice! He sounded just like the [116]deceased lady. He [117]casually asked them a [118]question, "Where is my husband? It is our [119]fortieth [120]wedding anniversary today!"

Chapter 5

Vocabulary

1. Manila [mə`nɪlə] 馬尼拉（菲律賓首都）

2. Philippines [`fɪləˌpinz] 菲律賓

3. ⁴amateur [`æməˌtʃur]（n.）業餘愛好者 （adj.）業餘的

4. ²musician [mju`zɪʃən]（n.）音樂家

5. ¹name [nem]（n.）名字；姓名 （v.）給……取名；給……命名 （phr.）①last name姓 ②middle name中名 ③first name名字

6. ²cancer [`kænsɚ]（n.）①癌症 ②（星座大寫）巨蟹座

7. ¹in ⁵agony（phr.）在極度痛苦中
   【相關字彙】
   ⁵agony [`ægənɪ]（n.）激烈的痛苦

8. proliferation [prəˌlɪfəˌreʃən]（n.）增加；擴散

9. ²cell [sɛl]（n.）①單人牢房 ②（生物）細胞 ③蜂房巢室

10. ⁴transfer [træns`fɝ]（v.）轉移；調動

11. ³clinic [`klɪnɪk]（n.）①診所 ②臨床講授 ③會診
    【相關字彙】
    ⁶clinical [`klɪnɪkl]（adj.）①臨床的 ②科學的；客觀的

12. ¹receive [rɪ`siv]（v.）①接受 ②收到 ③歡迎；招待 （phr.）receive sacraments 受聖餐 ☆ sacrament（n.）（常大寫）聖餐

【諺】It is more blessed to give than to receive.

　　　　施比受更有福。　blessed（adj.）受祝福的

13. [4]professional [prəˈfɛʃən!]（adj.）專業的　（n.）專家

【相關字彙】

[4]profession [prəˈfɛʃən]（n.）職業

14. [1]first [2]aid（phr.）急救

【相關字彙與重要片語】

[2]aid [ed]（n.）/（v.）幫助；援助　（phr.）①first-aid kit
急救箱　②come/go to Sb.'s aid 幫助某人

☆ [3]kit（n.）工具箱

15. [1]be [1]placed [1]in（phr.）被安置；被放置

16. [4]intensive [1]care [1]unit（phr.）加護病房

【相關字彙】

[4]intensive [ɪnˈtɛnsɪv]（adj.）①集中的；加強的　②特別護理的

[1]care [kɛr]（n.）/（v.）①注意；小心　②照顧；看護　③憂慮；關心；介意

【諺】Care killed the/a cat. 憂慮傷身。

[1]unit [ˈjunɪt]（n.）單位；單元

17. [5]ward [wɔrd]（n.）①underline{病房}　②選區　③保護；保衛　（v.）避開；避免　（phr.）ward off 擋開；避免

18. [1]move [1]into（phr.）搬入

19. [1]lie [laɪ]（n.）謊言　（v.）①underline{躺；臥}　②呈現……狀態；置

於 ③撒謊 （phr.）white lie 善意的謊言

【諺】As you make your bed, so you must <u>lie</u> in it.

自作自受；自食其果。

20. ³recover [rɪˋkʌvɚ] （v.）①<u>恢復；復原；痊癒</u> ②重獲

【相關字彙】

⁴recovery [rɪˋkʌvərɪ] （n.）①恢復；復原 ②重獲

21. ¹health [hɛlθ] （n.）健康 （phr.）health center 保健中心

【諺】He who has <u>health</u> has hope.

留得青山在，不怕沒柴燒。

【相關字彙】

²healthy [ˋhɛlθɪ] （adj.）健康的

22. ¹look ¹around（phr.）四處看；環顧

【相關字彙】

¹around [əˋraʊnd] （adv.）／（prep.）①四周；附近 ②圍繞

③大約……的時候

23. ²patient [ˋpeʃənt] （n.）<u>病人</u> （adj.）忍耐的 （phr.）be

patient with 對……有耐心

【相關字彙】

³patience [ˋpeʃəns] （n.）忍耐

24. obviously [ˋɑbvɪəslɪ] （adv.）明顯地

【相關字彙】

³obvious [ˋɑbvɪəs] （adj.）明白的；明顯的

25. ²drape [drep] （n.）窗簾；帷幔

26. ^{1}cover St. ^{1}up（phr.）遮掩某物

　　【相關字彙與重要片語】

　　^{1}cover ［`kʌvə］（v.）①覆蓋；包裹起 ②掩蔽 ③包含（n.）①遮蓋物 ②（書的）封面 （phr.）①take cover 隱蔽 ②under（the）cover of 在……掩護下

　　^{6}coverage ［`kʌvərɪdʒ］（n.）①覆蓋；覆蓋範圍 ②保險項目

27. ^{1}be ^{1}about ^{1}to（phr.）將要

28. ^{2}formal ［`fɔrml］（adj.）①<u>正式的</u> ②形式上的；外表上的 ③禮儀的

29. ^{6}diagnosis ［ˌdaɪəg`nosɪs］（n.）診斷；判斷

　　【相關字彙】

　　^{6}diagnose ［`daɪəgnoz］（v.）診斷

30. ^{3}announce ［ə`naʊns］（v.）通知；宣佈

31. ^{3}might ［maɪt］（aux.）<u>或許</u> （n.）力量

32. ^{1}make ^{1}it ^{2}through（phr.）渡過難關

33. ^{2}gentleman ［`dʒɛntlmən］（n.）紳士

34. ^{1}for ^{1}the ^{1}last ^{1}time（phr.）最後一次

35. ^{2}deliver ［dɪ`lɪvə］（v.）①投遞；傳送 ②<u>發表；宣佈；講</u> ③接生 （phr.）deliver oneself to the police 向警察自首

36. ^{1}news ［njuz］（n.）新聞；報導；<u>消息</u> （phr.）①make news 製造新聞 ②in the news 上了新聞 ③break the news to Sb. 把壞消息告訴某人

　　【諺】Good <u>news</u> goes on crutches, ill <u>news</u> flies apace.

好事不出門，壞事傳千里。 ^{3}crutch（n.）枴杖

^{2}ill（adj.）壞的　apace（adv.）急速地

37. ^{5}broth［brɔθ］（n.）（用肉、蔬菜等煮成的）清湯

38. ^{1}fall ^{2}asleep（phr.）睡著

39. nighttime［ˋnaɪtˌtaɪm］（n.）夜間

40. ^{4}physical［ˋfɪzɪk!］（adj.）①肉體的；身體的　②物質的　③物理學的　（phr.）physical education＝P.E. 體育

　☆ ^{2}education（n.）教育

41. ^{2}pain［pen］（v.）使痛苦　（n.）①痛苦；疼痛　②辛苦；努力　（phr.）（口）a pain in the neck 討人厭的人（或事物）

　【諺】No pains, no gains. 不勞則無獲。　 ^{2}gain（v.）獲得

42. ^{2}result ^{1}from（phr.）因……而產生

43. smoothly［ˋsmuðlɪ］（adv.）平靜地；安穩地

　【相關字彙】

　 ^{3}smooth［smuð］（adj.）①光滑的　②平靜的；平穩的　③流暢的　（v.）①使光滑　②使平靜；使和緩

44. ^{1}lie ^{1}half ^{3}awake（phr.）半睡半醒

　【相關字彙與重要片語】

　 ^{3}awake［əˋwek］（adj.）醒著的　（v.）①喚醒　②使覺醒　（phr.）awake to 意識到

45. constantly［ˋkɑnstəntlɪ］（adv.）①接連不斷地　②不變地

　【相關字彙】

　 ^{3}constant［ˋkɑnstənt］（adj.）①接連不斷的　②不變的

46. ¹back ¹and ³forth（phr.）來來回回地

　　【相關字彙】

　　³forth [forθ]（adv.）①向前 ②向外

47. ³burglar [ˋbɝglɚ]（n.）竊賊；強盜

48. ¹break ¹into（phr.）闖入

49. ²wonder [ˋwʌndɚ]（n.）①驚奇 ②奇觀 （v.）納悶；對……感到疑惑 （phr.）a nine day's wonder 曇花一現的人（或事物）

50. ¹do ¹not ¹have ¹a clue ¹about（phr.）關於……一無所知；毫無頭緒

　　【相關字彙】

　　³clue [klu]（n.）線索；頭緒

51. ⁴adjust [əˋdʒʌst]（v.）①調整 ②適應 （phr.）adjust oneself to 讓人適應

　　【相關字彙】

　　⁴adjustment [əˋdʒʌstmənt]（n.）調整；調節

52. ¹come ¹from（phr.）來自

53. ²cough [kɔf]（v.）/（n.）咳嗽

54. ³resist [rɪˋzɪst]（v.）①反抗；抵抗 ②耐；防

　　【相關字彙】

　　⁴resistance [rɪˋzɪstəns]（n.）抵抗力

　　⁶resistant [rɪˋzɪstənt]（adj.）抵抗的

55. ⁴curiosity [ˌkjʊrɪˋɑsətɪ]（n.）①好奇心 ②珍奇的事物

【相關字彙與重要片語】

²curious [ˈkjʊrɪəs]（adj.）①好奇的 ②奇怪的 （phr.）be curious about 對……有好奇心

56. ¹lift [lɪft]（v.）/（n.）舉起；抬起 （phr.）①lift up 舉起 ②give Sb. a lift 讓某人搭便車 ③thumb a lift 要求搭車

☆ ²thumb（n.）拇指

57. ²corner [ˈkɔrnə]（n.）角；街角 （phr.）①（商）corner the market 壟斷市場 ②cut corners（不按常規而）以簡便方法做事 ③drive/force/put Sb. into a corner 把某人逼上絕路

58. ²curtain [ˈkɜtn]（n.）①窗簾；帷幔 ②幕 （phr.）①lift/raise the curtain on 揭露 ②behind the curtain 祕密地

☆ ¹raise（v.）舉起

59. silently [ˈsaɪləntlɪ]（adv.）寂靜地；無聲地

【相關字彙】

²silent [ˈsaɪlənt]（adj.）①沉默的；無言的 ②寂靜的；無聲的

²silence [ˈsaɪləns]（n.）①沉默；無言 ②寂靜；無聲

60. motionlessly [ˈmoʃənlɪslɪ]（adv.）不動地；靜止地

【相關字彙】

²motion [ˈmoʃən]（n.）①運動；移動 ②動作

61. ³rely ¹on（phr.）依賴

【相關字彙】

³rely [rɪˈlaɪ]（v.）信賴；依賴

62. respirator [ˋrɛspəˌretɚ]（n.）呼吸器

63. ¹weak [wik]（adj.）①<u>弱的；虛弱的</u> ②軟弱的 （phr.）
①weak at（做事）拙於 ②weak point/side/spot 弱點；缺點
☆ ²spot（n.）汙點

【諺】The <u>weakest</u> goes to the wall. 弱肉強食。

64. ⁶fragile [ˋfrædʒəl]（adj.）①易碎的 ②<u>脆弱的</u>

65. ¹feel ²sleepy（phr.）想睡

66. ¹side ²effect（phr.）副作用

67. ²drug [drʌg]（n.）藥

68. ²function [ˋfʌŋkʃən]（n.）①功能；作用 ②職責；職務
（v.）①<u>起作用</u> ②（機器）工作；運作

【相關字彙】

⁴functional [ˋfʌŋkʃənḷ]（adj.）①機能的 ②起作用的

69. drastically [ˋdræstɪklɪ]（adv.）激烈地；猛烈地

【相關字彙】

⁶drastic [ˋdræstɪk]（adj.）①激烈的；猛烈的 ②嚴厲的；極
端的

70. ⁵gusts ¹of（phr.）（一）陣陣

【相關字彙】

⁵gust [gʌst]（n.）一陣 （v.）一陣陣地勁吹

71. freezing [ˋfrizɪŋ]（adj.）冰冷的；嚴寒的

【相關字彙】

³freeze [friz]（v.）①凍結；結冰 ②凍僵

72. ¹hit [hɪt]（n.）①打擊；命中 ②成功而風行一時的事物（v.）①打；揍 ②碰撞；撞上 ③襲擊（phr.）①hit the/one's books（拼命地）用功 ②hit the right nail on the head 一針見血 ③hit the hay/sack 就寢

☆ ²nail（n.）釘子 ³hay（n.）乾草 ³sack（n.）袋

73. intentionally [ɪnˈtɛnʃənlɪ]（adv.）企圖地；故意地
【相關字彙】
⁴intention [ɪnˈtɛnʃən]（n.）意圖
⁵intent [ɪnˈtɛnt]（n.）意圖；目的（adj.）①專心的；專注的 ②熱切的

74. partially [ˈpɑrʃəlɪ]（adv.）部分地
【相關字彙】
⁴partial [ˈpɑrʃəl]（adj.）①部分的 ②不公平的；偏愛的

75. ²alive [əˈlaɪv]（adj.）活的

76. ¹understand [ˌʌndəˈstænd]（v.）①理解；懂 ②認為；推斷 ③認識到；了解（phr.）make oneself understood 表達自己的意思

77. ⁶complexion [kəmˈplɛkʃən]（n.）臉色；面容

78. ⁶amiable [ˈemɪəbl̩]（adj.）①和藹可親的 ②友善的

79. ⁵hoarse [hɔrs]（adj.）嘶啞的

80. ¹voice [vɔɪs]（n.）聲音（v.）（用言語）表達；說出（phr.）①voice mail 語音信箱 ②lift up/raise one's voice 提高嗓門；抗議 ③with one voice 異口同聲地

81. ¹as ¹far ¹as Sb. ¹know（phr.）據某人所知

82. incurable [ɪnˋkjʊrəb!]（adj.）不能醫治的；無可救藥的

　　【相關字彙】

　　²cure [kjʊr]（v.）╱（n.）①治療 ②矯正

　　【諺】Prevention is better than <u>cure</u>. 預防勝於治療。

　　　　⁴prevention（n.）預防

83. ³disease [dɪˋziz]（n.）疾病

84. ³suppose [səˋpoz]（v.）①以爲；推測 ②<u>假定</u>

85. ³recover ¹from（phr.）從……恢復過來

86. ¹pay [pe]（v.）①支付；付款給 ②<u>付；付出代價</u> ③償還；
　　向……報復 （n.）①報酬；薪俸 ②報償；懲罰 （phr.）
　　①pay back 償還；報答 ②in the pay of 被……收買 ③pay
　　off 償清

　　【相關字彙】

　　¹payment [ˋpemənt]（n.）①支付；支付款 ②報償

87. ¹in ³exchange ¹for（phr.）交換

88. ¹of ¹course（phr.）當然

89. ³condition [kənˋdɪʃən]（n.）①狀態；情況 ②<u>條件</u> （phr.）
　　①on/upon condition that 只要；以……爲條件 ②on no
　　condition 決不

　　【相關字彙】

　　conditional [kənˋdɪʃən!]（adj.）有條件的；被限制的

90. ³harm [hɑrm]（n.）傷害；損害 （phr.）do Sb. harm 加害

某人

【相關字彙】

³harmful [ˈhɑrmfəl]（adj.）有害的

91. ³hesitate [ˈhɛzəˌtet]（v.）躊躇；猶豫

【相關字彙】

⁴hesitation [ˌhɛzəˈteʃən]（n.）躊躇；遲疑

92. ¹listen ¹to（phr.）注意聽

93. ¹important [ɪmˈpɔrtn̩t]（adj.）①<u>重要的</u> ②位尊的

94. ¹bring ¹up（phr.）①養育 ②<u>提出</u>

95. ¹in ²addition（phr.）另外

【相關字彙】

²addition [əˈdɪʃən]（n.）①加；附加 ②（數）加法

96. ⁶deliberate [dɪˈlɪbərɪt]（adj.）①深思熟慮的；慎重的 ②故意的（v.）<u>深思熟慮</u>

97. ⁵awhile [əˈhwaɪl]（adv.）片刻；一會兒

98. ⁵consent [kənˈsɛnt]（v.）/（n.）同意；答應（phr.）①consent to 同意；答應 ②age of consent（婚姻的）合法年齡

99. ¹that ¹is（phr.）換句話說

100. ¹make ¹a ²decision ¹for（phr.）為……做了一個決定

【相關字彙與重要片語】

¹decide [dɪˈsaɪd]（v.）決心；決定（phr.）decide on/upon 考慮後決定

⁶decisive〔dɪˋsaɪsɪv〕（adj.）①決定性的 ②堅決的

101. ¹make ¹up one's ¹mind（phr.）下定決心

【相關字彙與重要片語】

¹mind〔maɪnd〕（n.）①心；精神 ②理智 ③有頭腦（才智）的人　（v.）①留神；注意 ②介意；在乎　（phr.）①lose one's mind 發瘋 ②change one's mind 改變主意 ③bear/keep in mind 牢記　☆ ¹bear（v.）對……抱有

【諺】（All）great <u>minds</u> think alike. 英雄所見略同。

【諺】A contented <u>mind</u> is a perpetual feast. 知足常樂。

contented（adj.）滿足的　perpetual（adj.）永久的

102. ²whatever〔hwɑtˋɛvɚ〕（adj.）無論怎麼的　（pron.）<u>不論什麼</u>

103. ³suggest〔səˋdʒɛst〕（v.）①<u>建議</u> ②暗示 ③使聯想

【相關字彙與重要片語】

⁴suggestion〔səˋdʒɛstʃən〕（n.）①建議；提議 ②暗示 ③聯想（phr.）make/offer a suggestion 提議；建議

104. ¹reach ¹an ¹agreement ¹with Sb.（phr.）與某人達成協定（議）

105. ¹in ¹an ²instant（phr.）不久

【相關字彙與重要片語】

²instant〔ˋɪnstənt〕（adj.）①立刻的 ②緊急的 ③速食的；即溶的　（n.）瞬間；一刹那　（phr.）instant noodle 速食麵

106. ¹fall ¹into ¹a ¹deep ¹sleep（phr.）沉睡

107. ²exact〔ɪgˋzækt〕（adj.）確切的

108. heartbeat [ˈhɑrtˌbit]（n.）心跳

【相關字彙與重要片語】

¹beat [bit]（v.）①打；擊 ②擊敗；勝過 ③心跳 （n.）①
打；擊 ②心跳 ③拍子；節奏 （phr.）①be beat（口）筋疲
力盡地 ②beat one's brains（out）（口）絞盡腦汁 ③out of/
off Sb.'s beat 非某人本行

109. electrocardiogram [ɪˌlɛktroˈkɑrdɪəˌgræm]（n.）心電圖

110. ⁵wheelchair [ˈhwilˈtʃɛr]（n.）輪椅

111. ⁶subsequent ⁶consultation（phr.）複診

【相關字彙與重要片語】

⁶subsequent [ˈsʌbsɪˌkwɛnt]（adj.）後來的；隨後的

⁴consult [kənˈsʌlt]（v.）①看病；請教 ②商量 ③當顧問
（phr.）①consult with 商議 ②consult for 當顧問

⁶consultation [ˌkɑnsəlˈteʃən]（n.）①商量 ②診察

112. miraculously [məˈrækjələs]（adv.）奇蹟地

【相關字彙】

³miracle [ˈmɪrəkḷ]（n.）奇蹟

⁶miraculous [məˈrækjələs]（adj.）奇蹟的

113. ¹into ²thin ¹air（phr.）無影無蹤

【相關字彙與重要片語】

²thin [θɪn]（adj.）①薄的；細的；瘦的 ②稀疏的 ③稀薄
的 （v.）變細；變薄；變瘦 （phr.）①spread oneself thin
試圖同時做太多的工作 ②out of thin air 無中生有 ③（as）

thin as a rake（人）骨瘦如柴的

☆ ²spread（v.）延伸；展開　rake（n.）（長柄的）耙

114．³inform Sb.¹of St.（phr.）通知某人事情

【相關字彙】

³inform [ɪnˋfɔrm]（v.）通知；報告

⁴information [͵ɪnfɚˋmeʃən]（n.）①情報 ②資訊；知識

⁴informative [ɪnˋfɔrmətɪv]（adj.）①情報的 ②見聞廣博的 ③教育性的

115．⁴horrify [ˋhɔrə͵faɪ]（v.）使恐懼；使驚懼

116．deceased [dɪˋsist]（adj.）已故的

【相關字彙】

decease [dɪˋsis]（n.）/（v.）死亡

117．casually [ˋkæʒjuəlɪ]（adv.）無意地

【相關字彙】

³casual [ˋkæʒuəl]（adj.）①偶然的 ②隨便的 ③臨時的

118．¹question [ˋkwɛstʃən]（n.）①問題 ②疑問　（v.）①質問 ②懷疑　（phr.）①beyond/without/past question 毫無疑問 ②there's no question of ……是不可能的

【諺】There are two sides to every question.

公說公有理，婆說婆有理。

119．fortieth [ˋfɔrtɪɪθ]（n.）/（adj.）第四十（的）

120．¹wedding ⁴anniversary（phr.）結婚紀念日

【相關字彙】

[1]wedding [ˈwɛdɪŋ]（n.）婚禮

[4]anniversary [ˌænəˈvɝsərɪ]（n.）（每年的）紀念日

～ 第六章 ～
波音666

根據很多年前廣播（²broadcast）的新聞報導，FBI曾經對眾人揭露（³reveal）一件可怕的事件。波音客機（Boeing）666班機（²flight），正飛往一個傳說的（⁶legendary）、惡名昭彰的（⁶notorious）地方——百慕達三角洲，也稱為惡魔（³devil）三角，在那裡一再發生（recurrent）很多有關人們神祕的死亡，和意外（³accident）失蹤的謎（³mystery）樣的事。突然，這架飛機上的人們與在佛羅里達州（Florida）的地面塔台失去了聯繫，而飛機，毫無任何前兆，以這樣如謎的（enigmatic）方式消失了。

這架飛機，如那樣沒有建立（⁴establish）任何的聯繫，不見（gone）了。經過四天三夜之後，無預期

～ Chapter 6 ～
The Boeing 666

According to the news report [1]broadcasted many years ago, the FBI once [2]revealed a scary incident to the public. The [3]Boeing 666 [4]Flight was [5]flying to a [6]legendary and [7]notorious place, [8]the Bermuda Triangle, also, called the [9]Devil's Triangle, where many [10]mysteries about [11]recurrent and mysterious deaths and disappearances of people in [12]accidents took place. Suddenly, people on the flight [13]lost contact with the [14]airport tower on the ground in the State of [15]Florida, and the flight, without any warning seemed to disappear [16]in such an [17]enigmatic way.

Just like that, the plane, without [18]establishing any contact, was [19]gone. After four days and three nights, a few [20]signals were

地（unexpectedly），從飛機（²aircraft）上再次間歇地（periodically）對塔台發出（⁵issue）了一些信號（³signal）。而飛機上的人們聯繫了塔台，請求（³request）緊急降落（landing）至一條安全航道上。

很快地，由於此危急的（⁴desperate）狀況，所有飛機塔台人員（⁵personnel）最終（eventually）允許（¹allow）了飛機降落於較遠的右邊的機場跑道（runway）上。說來也奇怪，等到飛機降落後，飛機就好似一名躺在停屍間（mortuary）的死人。也就是說，飛機異常安靜地矗立在那裡。飛機的艙門依然緊閉著，沒有讓任何一人可以進入的樣子。經過很久的時間，飛機仍是（³remain）靜止的（static）停留於地面之上，也沒有任何關於在飛機上為何無人將會打開艙門的線索。

[21]unexpectedly [22]issued [23]periodically from the [24]aircraft again to the tower. And the people on the plane contacted the tower and [25]requested an emergency [26]landing on a safe path.

Soon, [27]thanks to the [28]desperate situation, all airport tower [29]personnel [30]eventually [31]allowed the plane to land on the far right side of the [32]runway. [33]Strangely enough, after the plane landed, it was just like a dead person lying in a [34]mortuary. That is, the plane stood there very quietly. The cabin doors were still closed, not [35]accessible to anybody. The plane [36]remained [37]static on the ground [38]for a very long time; there were not any clues about why no one on the plane would open the doors, either.

　　因此（consequently），航警與消防員（firefighter）試著用盡他們全部的力氣（³strength），使用不同種類的（³various）工具（¹tool），很有效率地（efficiently）去將艙門開鎖（⁶unlock）。就在一座艙的第一扇艙門被打開了之後，一股怪異、令人厭惡的（⁵nasty）臭味接踵而來（ensue）使他們感到噁心。接下來，戲劇性地（dramatically），飛機上一個毛骨悚然的景象（¹sight）使他們大吃了一驚，就好像是他們的魂魄（¹soul）出了竅一般。人們無法想像（²imagine）飛機上發生了什麼樣的混亂（⁶chaos）。他們看到很多乘客的屍體到處散佈（³scatter）在分別不同的（²separate）座艙之中。飛機上的人們全都死了！在屍體（⁶corpse）之中，他們發現到一張身分證（⁴ID）在地面上，靠近一名死者的口袋。他事實上是一位政治的（³political）候選人（⁴candidate）。他也是一位機智的（⁶witty）人，擁有很大膽量（⁵guts）。在最近的（²latest）紐約新聞關於他的報導中，他死前都一直正在競選紐約市長的（mayoral）職位（¹position）。

[39]Consequently, the [40]airport police and [41]firefighters tried to [42]use up all their [43]strength to [44]unlock the doors with [45]various [46]tools very [47]efficiently. Just after the first door of one cabin was opened, an odd and [48]nasty smell [49]ensued, and it [50]turned their stomachs. Then, [51]dramatically, the horrible [52]sight on the plane [53]took their breath away; it was like their [54]souls were coming out of the bodies. People could not [55]imagine what [56]chaos had taken place on the plane. They saw that many of the passengers' bodies were [57]scattered everywhere in the [58]separate cabins. The people on the plane were all dead! Among the [59]corpses, they found [60]ID on the ground, near a dead person's pocket. He was actually a [61]political [62]candidate. He was also a [63]witty person with [64]plenty of [65]guts. The [66]latest news about him in New York was that he had been [67]running for the New York [68]mayoral [69]position before his death.

當他們更進入到飛機裡邊，移動時，又看到有一些像是燒焦的（burnt），被一場大火燒烤（⁴broil）過的屍體。似乎有的屍體還是冰凍的（frozen），或者被噴出（⁶eruption）的血液覆蓋住。另外，還有屍體噁心的（disgusting）的部分像是被剁細（³chop）成了肉（¹meat）醬（²sauce）。這飛機上場面真使他們恐懼！換句話說，飛機上所發生的差不多似乎是一場殘酷的（⁵savage）、無人性的（inhumane）大屠殺（⁶massacre）啊！

　　每個人都非常不明白的是：關於飛機上發生了什麼事。意外前，是誰駕駛著飛機呢？既然這樣，飛安專家收回（⁶retrieve）了什麼是飛機上最具重要性的黑盒子，並且回去對它做一些例行的檢驗（²test）。他們希望能找出一個合理的（³reasonable）解釋（⁴explanation），或是甚至是找出發生此可怕事件的答案。

When they moved further into the plane, they also saw some bodies which seemed to be [70]burnt or [71]broiled by a big fire. It seemed some bodies were [72]frozen or [73]covered with an [74]eruption of blood. [75]What's more; there were [76]disgusting body parts which appeared to be [77]chopped into [78]meat [79]sauce. The scene on the plane really horrified them! [80]In other words, what happened on the plane was almost like a [81]savage and [82]inhumane [83]massacre.

Everyone wondered a lot about what had happened on the plane. Who had flown the aircraft before the accident? Then, the flight safety experts [84]retrieved what was [85]of the utmost importance — the [86]flight recorder on the airplane — and [87]went back to do some routine [88]tests on it. They hoped to find a [89]reasonable [90]explanation or even the answer to this horrible incident.

　　首先，從黑盒子聽到的，好像是傳來機長（²captain）的聲音。隨即（thereupon）並也聽見機長的宣佈（³announcement）：「我們應該完全進入（²entrance）一層異常的（unusual）迷霧（¹fog）之中。不！可能是一種危險的（²dangerous）氣流（airflow）。請趕快回到您的座位上，並且繫緊（³fasten）您的安全帶。」在一長段時間無聲之後，黑盒子就沒有產生（²produce）任何其它的聲音了。

　　隨著時間一分一秒地過去，大家流言蜚語（³gossip）說著，更多有關最後飛機上乘客遭遇（⁶undergo）的事情。此時，從黑盒子傳來，有一個喧鬧的聲音，彷彿是在降落前飛機上的人們正身處於一種一團亂的情況之中：猛烈地（fiercely）尖叫、吵架和打架著。又在黑盒子裡人們聽見了一個極大、非常刺耳的（⁴harsh）聲響。同一時間，從一名飛機上無法認出的（unrecognized）人嘴裡，一個聲音微弱地（dimly）被聽出來

First, it sounded like the [91]captain's voice was coming from the flight recorder. [92]Thereupon, the captain's [93]announcement was also heard: "We should complete the [94]entrance into [95]a curtain of [96]unusual [97]fog. No! It may be a kind of [98]dangerous [99]airflow. Please quickly go back to your seats and [100]fasten your [101]seat belts well." After [102]a long period of silence, the flight recorder did not [103]produce any other sounds.

As time [104]went by, everyone [105]gossiped more about what the passengers had [106]undergone on the aircraft [107]in the end. At this point, from the flight recorder, there was a sound of [108]hustle and bustle coming out as if people on the plane had been screaming, quarreling, and fighting [109]fiercely [110]in a state of chaos before landing. Also on the flight recorder, people heard a very loud and [111]harsh sound. At the same time, a voice was

了。他說出話來：「你們知道我們曾經去過哪裡嗎？我們去了地獄（³hell）。」

[112]dimly heard from an [113]unrecognizable person on the plane. He [114]spoke out, "Do you know where we've been? We [115]have been to '[116]Hell.' "

Chapter 6

Vocabulary

1. ²broadcast [ˈbrɔdˌkæst]（v.）/（n.）廣播

2. ³reveal [rɪˈvil]（v.）①顯露出 ②揭露；揭示 （phr.）reveal oneself 表明身分；講出姓名

   【相關字彙】

   ⁶revelation [rɛvlˈeʃən]（n.）暴露；意想不到的事

3. Boeing [ˈboɪŋ]（n.）波音客機

4. ²flight [flaɪt]（n.）①飛翔 ②飛機

5. ¹fly ¹to（phr.）飛往

6. ⁶legendary [ˈlɛdʒndˌɛrɪ]（adj.）傳說的；傳奇的

   【相關字彙】

   ⁴legend [ˈlɛdʒnd]（n.）傳說；傳奇故事

7. ⁶notorious [noˈtorɪəs]（adj.）惡名昭彰的

8. ¹the Bermuda ²Triangle　百慕達三角洲（地名）

9. ³devil [ˈdɛvl]（n.）惡魔；魔鬼

10. ³mystery [ˈmɪstərɪ]（n.）謎；神祕；不可思議的事

11. recurrent [rɪˈkɜənt]（adj.）一再發生的；循環的

    【相關字彙與重要片語】

    ³current　[ˈkɜənt]（adj.）①流行的 ②最新的 ③現在的 （n.）①流動 ②思潮；趨勢 （phr.）swim with/against the

current 順應／違反 潮流

[5]currency [ˈkɝənsɪ]（n.）①通貨；貨幣 ②流通；通用

12. [3]accident [ˈæksədənt]（n.）事故；災禍；意外事件 （phr.）

by accident 意外地

【諺】Accidents will happen.

天有不測風雲，人有旦夕禍福。

【相關字彙】

[4]accidental [ˌæksəˈdɛntl]（adj.）偶然的；意外的

13. [2]lose [2]contact [1]with（phr.）失去聯繫

【相關字彙與重要片語】

[2]lose [luz]（v.）①遺失 ②輸；失敗 ③迷失 （phr.）①lose one's way 迷路 ②lose one's tongue 張口結舌；說不出話來

【諺】Grasp all, lose all. 貪者必失。 [3]grasp（v.）抓牢

[2]loser [ˈluzɚ]（n.）失敗者

[2]loss [lɔs]（n.）①喪失 ②虧損 ③失敗；輸 （phr.）loss of face 丟臉

lost [lɔst]（adj.）①弄丟的 ②迷路的 （phr.）be lost in St. 全神貫注；沉浸於

【諺】Learning without thought is labor lost; thought without learning is perilous. 學而不思則罔，思而不學則殆。

perilous（adj.）危險的

[2]contact [ˈkɑntækt]（n.）／（v.）①接觸 ②聯繫 （phr.）in contact with 與……有聯繫

14. ¹airport ²tower（phr.）機場塔台

15. Florida [`flɔrədə] 佛羅里達州（美國州名）

16. ¹in ¹a（n）…¹way（phr.）以……的方式

17. enigmatic [ˌɛnɪgˋmætɪk]（adj.）如謎的；難理解的
【相關字彙】
enigma [ɪˋnɪgmə]（n.）謎；難以理解的人（或事物）

18. ⁴establish [əˋstæblɪʃ]（v.）建立；創立
【相關字彙】
⁴establishment [əsˋtæblɪʃmənt]（n.）建立；創立

19. gone [gɔn]（adj.）①死去的 ②不見的

20. ³signal [ˋsɪgnḷ]（n.）①信號；暗號 ②標誌 （v.）以信號告
知；以手勢示意

21. unexpectedly [ˌʌnɪkˋspɛktɪdlɪ]（adv.）無預期地；出乎意料地

22. ⁵issue [ˋɪʃʊ]（v.）①發行；出版 ②發出 （n.）議題 （phr.）
①at issue 爭議中的 ②face the issue 面對事實 ③make an issue
of 挑起爭議

23. periodically [ˌpɪrɪˋɑdɪklɪ]（adv.）定期地；間歇地
【相關字彙】
periodical [ˌpɪrɪˋɑdɪkḷ]（n.）定期刊物；雜誌 （adj.）定期
地；間歇地

24. ²aircraft [ˋɛrˌkræft]（n.）飛行器

25. ³request [rɪˋkwɛst]（n.）/（v.）請求；請願 （phr.）①at
Sb.'s request 應某人的要求 ②to request a favor 求情

☆ ²favor（n.）恩惠

26. landing [ˈlændɪŋ]（n.）降落；登陸

27. ¹thanks ¹to（phr.）由於

28. ⁴desperate [ˈdɛspərɪt]（adj.）①危急的 ②鋌而走險的 ③渴望
獲得……的

29. ⁵personnel [ˌpɝsn̩ˈɛl]（n.）（總稱）人員

30. eventually [ɪˈvɛntʃʊəlɪ]（adv.）最終地
【相關字彙】
⁴eventual [ɪˈvɛntʃʊəl]（adj.）結果的；最後的

31. ¹allow Sb. ¹to ¹do（phr.）允許某人做
【相關字彙】
¹allow [əˈlaʊ]（v.）允許；讓
⁴allowance [əˈlaʊəns]（n.）（定期的）津貼；零用錢

32. runway [ˈrʌnˌwe]（n.）機場跑道

33. strangely ¹enough（phr.）十分奇怪地

34. mortuary [ˈmɔrtʃʊˌɛrɪ]（n.）停屍間

35. (¹be) ⁶accessible ¹to（phr.）可接近的；可進入的
【相關字彙】
⁴access [ˈæksɛs]（n.）①接近；進入 ②入口
⁶accessible [ækˈsɛsəbl̩]（adj.）①易接近的 ②容易取得的

36. ³remain [rɪˈmen]（v.）①留下；剩下 ②仍是；保持 ③逗留

37. static [ˈstætɪk]（adj.）靜止的；不動的

38. ¹for ¹a ¹very ¹long ¹time（phr.）很長（久）的時間

39. consequently [ˈkɑnsəˌkwɛntlɪ]（adv.）因此；所以

【相關字彙與重要片語】

⁴consequent [ˈkɑnsəˌkwɛnt]（adj.）起因於

⁴consequence [ˈkɑnsəˌkwɛns]（n.）①結果 ②重要 （phr.）

in consequence of 由於

40. ¹airport ¹police（phr.）航警

41. firefighter [ˈfaɪrˌfaɪtə]（n.）消防員

42. ¹use ¹up（phr.）用完

43. ³strength [strɛnθ]（n.）力量；氣力

44. ⁶unlock [ʌnˈlɑk]（v.）開……的鎖

45. ³various [ˈvɛrɪəs]（adj.）各式各樣的；不同種類的

【相關字彙與重要片語】

³variety [vəˈraɪətɪ]（n.）①多變化；多樣性 ②種類 （phr.）

a variety of 許多種的

³vary [ˈvɛrɪ]（v.）變化

46. ¹tool [tul]（n.）工具

47. efficiently [ɪˈfɪʃəntlɪ]（adv.）有效率地

【相關字彙】

³efficient [ɪˈfɪʃənt]（adj.）①有效率的 ②有能力的

48. ⁵nasty [ˈnæstɪ]（adj.）令人厭惡的；令人作嘔的

49. ensue [ɛnˈsu]（v.）隨後發生；接踵而來

50. ¹turn one's ²stomach（phr.）讓人反感（或噁心）

【相關字彙與重要片語】

²stomach [ˋstʌmək]（n.）胃 （phr.）①have no stomach for 對……沒有胃口；對……沒有興趣 ②have butterflies in one's stomach 緊張

☆ ¹butterfly（n.）蝴蝶

51. dramatically [drəˋmætɪk!ɪ]（adv.）戲劇地
   【相關字彙】
   ²drama [ˋdrɑmə]（n.）戲劇
   ³dramatic [drəˋmætɪk]（adj.）戲劇的

52. ¹sight [saɪt]（n.）①景象 ②看見 ③視力 （phr.）①at （the）sight of 一看見 ②out of sight 看不見 ③lose sight of 不再看見
   【諺】Out of sight, out of mind. 離久則情疏。
   【相關字彙】
   ⁴sightseeing [ˋsaɪtˏsiɪŋ]（n.）觀光；遊覽

53. ¹take one's ³breath ¹away（phr.）大吃一驚

54. ¹soul [sol]（n.）①靈魂；魂魄 ②精神 （phr.）soul mate 情人；性情相投的人 ☆ ²mate（n.）配偶

55. ²imagine [ɪˋmædʒɪn]（v.）想像
   【相關字彙】
   ³imagination [ɪˏmædʒəˋneʃən]（n.）想像力

56. ⁶chaos [ˋkeɑs]（n.）混亂狀態；混沌

57. ³scatter [ˋskætɚ]（v.）①散佈；撒播 ②驅散；消除

58. ²separate [ˋsɛpəˏret]（adj.）分開的；個別的 （v.）使分開

（phr.）be separated from 使分離

【相關字彙】

^{3}separation [ˌsɛpəˈreʃən]（n.）分離

59. ^{6}corpse [kɔrps]（n.）屍體

60. ^{4}identification/ ^{4}ID [aɪˌdɛntəfəˈkeʃən]/[ˈaɪˈdi]（n.）①認出；識別；確認 ②身分證

61. ^{3}political [pəˈlɪtɪkl̩]（adj.）政治的 （phr.）political asylum 政治庇護 ☆ ^{6}asylum（n.）避難（所）；庇護權

【相關字彙】

^{3}politics [ˈpɑlətɪks]（n.）政治（學）

62. ^{4}candidate [ˈkændədet]（n.）①候選人 ②考生

63. ^{6}witty [ˈwɪtɪ]（adj.）①機智的 ②詼諧的

【相關字彙與重要片語】

^{4}wit [wɪt]（n.）①智力 ②機智 ③風趣 （phr.）①at one's wits' end 窮於應付；不知所措 ②live by one's wits 靠小聰明混日子

64. ^{3}plenty ^{1}of（phr.）很多的

【相關字彙】

^{3}plenty [ˈplɛntɪ]（n.）多量；多數

65. ^{5}gut [gʌt]（n.）①腸子 ②內臟（複數） ③（口）膽量（複數） （v.）取出內臟 （phr.）have the guts 有膽量

66. ^{2}latest [ˈletɪst]（adj.）最近的；最新的

67. ^{1}run ^{1}for（phr.）競選

68. mayoral ['meərəl]（adj.）市長的

　　【相關字彙】

　　³mayor ['meɚ]（n.）市長

69. ¹position [pə'zɪʃən]（n.）①位置；場所 ②職位 ③立場；態度

70. burnt [bɝnt]（adj.）燒焦的

71. ⁴broil [brɔɪl]（v.）烤；炙

72. frozen ['frozn̩]（adj.）冰凍

73. ¹be ¹covered ¹with（phr.）被……覆蓋

74. ⁶eruption [ɪ'rʌpʃən]（n.）爆發；噴出

　　【相關字彙】

　　⁵erupt [ɪ'rʌpt]（v.）噴出；爆發

75. what's ¹more（phr.）而且；此外

76. disgusting [dɪs'gʌstɪŋ]（adj.）噁心的

　　【相關字彙與重要片語】

　　⁴disgust [dɪs'gʌst]（n.）厭惡；嫌惡 （v.）使討厭；使嫌惡
　　（phr.）be/feel disgusted at/by/with 對……感到厭惡

77. ³chop [tʃɑp]（v.）①砍；劈 ②切碎；剁細 （phr.）①chop
　　down 砍倒 ②chop into 插話

78. ¹meat [mit]（n.）肉類 （phr.）meat and potatoes（俚）最
　　重要或基本的部分 ☆ ²potato（n.）馬鈴薯

79. ²sauce [sɔs]（n.）調味醬；醬汁

　　【諺】What's <u>sauce</u> for the goose is sauce for the gander.

一視同仁。 ¹goose（n.）雌鵝　gander（n.）雄鵝

【諺】The <u>sauce</u> is better than the fish.

喧賓奪主；本末倒置。

80. ¹in ¹other ¹words（phr.）換句話說

81. ⁵savage [`sævɪdʒ]（adj.）①野蠻的；未開化的 ②<u>殘酷的；兇</u><u>猛的</u>（n.）野蠻人

82. inhumane [͵ɪnhjuˋmen]（adj.）無人性的；殘忍的

【相關字彙】

¹human [ˋhjumən]（adj.）①人類的 ②有人性的　（n.）人

⁴humanity [hjuˋmænɪtɪ]（n.）人性

83. ⁶massacre [ˋmæsəkɚ]（n.）/（v.）大屠殺；殘殺

84. ⁶retrieve [rɪˋtriv]（v.）①<u>重新得到；收回</u> ②挽回；彌補 ③復活

85. ¹of ¹the ⁶utmost ²importance（phr.）極為重要

【相關字彙】

⁶utmost [ˋʌt͵most]（adj.）①極度的 ②最遠的 ③最大的（n.）最大限度

86. ²flight ³recorder（phr.）飛機黑盒子

【相關字彙】

³recorder [rɪˋkɔrdɚ]（n.）①錄音機 ②記錄者（器）

87. ¹go ¹back ¹to（phr.）返回

88. ²test [tɛst]（n.）/（v.）測驗；檢驗　（phr.）①put to the test 使受試驗（或考驗）②stand the test 經得起考驗

【諺】Misfortune <u>tests</u> the sincerity of friends. 患難見眞情。
⁴misfortune（n.）不幸　⁴sincerity（n.）眞實

89. ³reasonable [ˈriznəbl̩]（adj.）①<u>合理的</u> ②理智的 ③公道的

90. ⁴explanation [ˌɛkspləˈneʃən]（n.）①<u>說明；解釋</u> ②辯明；辯解

91. ²captain [ˈkæptɪn]（n.）①隊長；船長；<u>機長</u> ②陸軍上尉；海軍上校

92. thereupon [ˌðɛrəˈpɑn]（adv.）①<u>隨即；立即</u> ②於是；因此

93. ³announcement [əˈnaʊnsmənt]（n.）宣佈；公佈　（phr.）make an announcement of 宣佈

94. ²entrance [ˈɛntrəns]（n.）①入口；大門 ②<u>進入；入學；入場</u>

【相關字彙與重要片語】

¹enter [ˈɛntɚ]（v.）進入　（phr.）enter into ①加入；開始 ②成爲……的一部分 ③考慮；討論

95. ¹a ²curtain ¹of（phr.）一層

96. unusual [ʌnˈjuʒʊəl]（adj.）異常的；奇怪的

97. ¹fog [fɑg]（n.）霧；濃霧；煙霧　（phr.）in a fog 困惑的

【相關字彙】

²foggy [ˈfɑgɪ]（adj.）有濃霧的

98. ²dangerous [ˈdendʒərəs]（adj.）危險的

【諺】A little learning is a <u>dangerous</u> thing.
一知半解是危險的。

99. airflow [ˋɛrˏflo]（n.）氣流

100. ³fasten [ˋfæsn̩]（v.）繫緊

101. ¹seat ²belt（phr.）安全帶

【相關字彙與重要片語】

²belt [bɛlt]（n.）①腰帶；帶 ②（常大寫）地帶；地區（phr.）tighten one's belt 束緊腰帶度日

☆ ³tighten（v.）使變緊

102. ¹a ²period ¹of（phr.）一段時間（期）

【相關字彙與重要片語】

²period [ˋpɪrɪəd]（n.）①一段時間；時期 ②（美）句號 ③（一堂）課；課時 （phr.）put a period to 使結束

103. ²produce [prəˋdjus]（v.）生產；產生

【相關字彙】

²producer [prəˋdjusɚ]（n.）製作者

104. ¹go ¹by（phr.）時間流逝

105. ³gossip [ˋgɑsəp]（n.）閒話 （v.）說閒話；流言蜚語

106. ⁶undergo [ˏʌndɚˋgo]（v.）遭受；遭遇

107. ¹in ¹the ¹end（phr.）最終

108. hustle ¹and bustle（phr.）喧鬧聲

109. fiercely [ˋfɪrslɪ]（adv.）猛烈地；狂暴地

【相關字彙】

⁴fierce [fɪrs]（adj.）①凶猛的 ②猛烈的；狂暴的

110. ¹in ¹a ¹state ¹of（phr.）在……的狀況

111. [4]harsh [hɑrʃ]（adj.）①刺耳的 ②粗糙的 ③嚴厲的

112. dimly [ˋdɪmlɪ]（adv.）微弱地

【相關字彙】

[3]dim [dɪm]（adj.）①微暗的 ②朦朧的；模糊的 （v.）使微暗；使模糊

113. unrecognizable [ʌnˋrɛkəɡˏnaɪzəb!]（adj.）無法認出的

【相關字彙】

[3]recognize [ˋrɛkəɡˏnaɪz]（v.）認出；認得；承認

114. [1]speak [1]out（phr.）說出

115. [1]have been [1]to（phr.）曾經去過

116. [3]hell [hɛl]（n.）地獄

~ 第七章 ~
# 一二三木頭人

有一個在我們的童年（³childhood）裡流行的有趣的（interesting）遊戲（¹game），那就叫做一二三木頭人。很多人小孩時都喜歡和他們的玩伴（playmate）玩這個遊戲。當我在台灣的台東縣讀小學時，大約是十五年前，我也喜歡一二三木頭人的遊戲。但是，我也因為這個遊戲而付出了慘痛的代價（¹price）。那是一個悲傷的經驗，造成我日後終生變得自閉的（autistic），因為，玩此遊戲時我受到了異常的驚嚇。

那時是春天，很多鬱金香（³tulip）和櫻花樹正開始開花（⁴bloom）了。在一次機會（⁴occasion）裏，我隔壁的（¹next-¹door）其中一位鄰居，一位叫做阿武的小孩，我們都覺得十

∽ Chapter 7 ∾
Red Light, Green Light

There was an [1]interesting [2]game which [3]caught on in my [4]childhood, that was called, "[5]red light, green light." Many people liked to play the game with their [6]playmates as kids. When I studied in [7]primary school in [8]Taitung County, Taiwan, about fifteen years ago, I was [9]fond of the game red light, green light, too. But I also paid a painful [10]price because of it. That sad experience later [11]resulted in me becoming [12]autistic [13]for life because I had gotten unusually frightened while playing the game.

It was spring; many [14]tulips and [15]cherry blossoms were beginning to [16]bloom. On one [17]occasion, one of my [18]next-door neighbors, a child, named A-wu, and I were both very bored,

分無聊，所以計畫一起去玩一二三木頭人的遊戲。我們也約定好，輸的人將會請贏的人（²winner）喝一瓶飲料（⁶beverage）。玩了剪刀、石頭、布的遊戲之後，我輸了。所以，我用手遮掩住我的眼睛且開始大聲喊叫（¹shout）了起來。我並立刻轉身，而看到阿武在我後方不動的樣子。接下來，我再次做了同樣的事。在第二次的時候，我迅速地往後看，並且看見阿武的腳緊緊地黏住地面的樣子；但是，這一次他所站住的地方似乎很怪異。它看起來像是一座原住民的（⁶aboriginal）墓地（⁶cemetery），被形形色色圖案（²pattern）的圖騰（totem）、刺青（tattoo），還有異國風情的（⁶exotic）羽毛（³feather）圍繞著。

當他繼續（¹continue）待在那不吉利（unlucky）的地方時，阿武這才真正地惹惱了我。我警告（³warn）他說：「我必須中斷（³pause）這場遊戲。我不想繼續這比賽（⁴competition）的事情（³stuff）了。」然後，我喋喋不休地說（⁵chatter）著關

so we [19]decided to play the game red light, green light together. We also [20]made a deal; the loser would buy the [21]winner a [22]beverage. After playing [23]paper, scissors, stone, I lost. So, I covered my eyes with my hands and started to [24]shout loudly. And immediately, I turned and saw A—wu motionless behind me. Next, I did the same thing again. For the second time, I looked back very quickly and saw A—wu's feet [25]stick to the ground, but the place where he stood this time appeared very strange. It looked like an [26]aboriginal [27]cemetery surrounded by various [28]patterns of [29]totems, [30]tattoos, and [31]exotic [32]feathers.

A—wu really [33]rubbed me the wrong way when he [34]continued to stay in that [35]unlucky place. I [36]warned him, "I have to [37]pause the game. I do not want to [38]carry on with this [39]competition [40]stuff." Then, I [41]chattered [42]on and on about

於阿武如何實在是不應該仍然站在那裡，在那詭異的、圓形的（⁴circular）小丘旁邊。當更靠近過去檢查那區域，在額外（²extra）、仔細的（⁵cautious）觀察（⁴observation）之後，我發現到它其實是一座無名（unnamed）墓。

此刻，正是美麗夕陽（sunset）西沉的時候。在這麼荒涼（⁶bleak）之地，到處都有蟋蟀（³cricket）伴隨著一些像狼嗥叫（⁵howl）的狗叫聲音。過了一會兒，阿武起鬨說：「請讓我們繼續玩這項遊戲吧！現在尚未是決定（³determine）誰是贏家的時候呢！」我無法抗拒阿武的要求，而答應了他，我們將會玩完一二三木頭人的遊戲的最後這一回合（¹round）。雖然感覺不舒服，我最後一次大聲地叫著。

how A-wu should really not still stand there, beside that weird and ⁴³circular hill. After some ⁴⁴extra ⁴⁵cautious ⁴⁶observations as I came closer to ⁴⁷check out the area, I found that it was ⁴⁸in fact an ⁴⁹unnamed tomb.

At the moment, ⁵⁰it was time for a beautiful ⁵¹sunset. The sound of ⁵²crickets was everywhere ⁵³along with some wolf-like ⁵⁴howls of dogs in this ⁵⁵bleak place. After a while, A-wu ⁵⁶kicked up a fuss and said, "Let's ⁵⁷get on with the game, please! It is not time yet to ⁵⁸determine who the winner is!" I ⁵⁹failed to resist A-wu's request, and promised him we would complete the final ⁶⁰round of the game red light, green light. Though I was ⁶¹under the weather, I shouted loudly for the last time.

這一次，轉過身來時，我留意到某個在身後令我感到毛骨悚然的東西。我往後看之後，看來好像在黑暗中有兩個影子：一個是站在離開我比較遠的（³farther）阿武，而另外一個被辨識（⁴identify）成像是，一個幽靈般的（shadowy）怪物（²monster），他緊鄰著一棵樹。這怪物幾乎就要緊抓住我朋友和他的背包（⁴backpack），而此怪物停止不動著。怪物像是想要和我們一起玩一二三木頭人的遊戲。實際上，他看起來稍微（³somewhat）像是一隻原住民的鬼。他有一張血淋淋的（²bloody）、極醜陋的（hideous）、扭曲的（distorted）臉孔，他身上穿戴（¹wear）其族群鮮豔的、象徵性的（⁶symbolic）裝飾品（⁴decoration）。那時候，他還向我們露出孩子般的（²childlike）微笑。

This time when I had [62]turned around, I [63]kept an eye on something behind me which [64]made my blood run cold. It appeared that there were two shadows in the dark after I looked back: one was A—wu standing [65]farther away from me, and the other was [66]identified as a [67]shadowy [68]monster, which was [69]adjacent to a tree. The monster—like thing almost [70]clung to my friend and his [71]backpack, and he stopped moving. It seemed that he wanted to play the game red light, green light with us. Actually, the monster looked [72]somewhat like an aboriginal ghost. He had a [73]bloody, [74]hideous, and [75]distorted face and was [76]wearing some colorful [77]symbolic [78]decorations of his tribe on his body. At that time, he also showed a [79]childlike smile to us.

Chapter 7

Vocabulary

1. interesting [ˈɪntərɪstɪŋ] (adj.) 有趣的

    【相關字彙與重要片語】

    ¹interest [ˈɪntərɪst] (n.) ①興趣；愛好；嗜好 ②利益 (v.) 使感興趣；使關心 (phr.) be interested in 對……有興趣

2. ¹game [gem] (n.) ①遊戲 ②競賽 ③獵物 (phr.) ①play the game 辦事公正；為人正直 ②have the game in one's hands 穩操勝算

    【諺】Lookers-on see most of the game.

      當局者迷，旁觀者清。

3. ¹catch ¹on (phr.) 流行

    【相關字彙與重要片語】

    ¹catch [kætʃ] (v.) ①逮住；捕獲 ②抓住；接住 ③趕上 (phr.) catch up with 趕上

    【諺】A drowning man will catch a straw。 急不暇擇。

      ³drown (v.) 溺死 ²straw (n.) 稻草

4. ³childhood [ˈtʃaɪldˌhʊd] (n.) 童年時期

5. ¹red ¹light ¹green ¹light (phr.) (遊戲) 一二三木頭人

6. playmate [ˈpleˌmet] (n.) 玩伴

7. [3]primary [1]school（phr.）小學

　　【相關字彙】

　　[3]primary [ˋpraɪͺmɛrɪ]（adj.）①第一的；主要的　②初步的；初級的　③基本的；根本的

8. Taitung [2]County 台東縣（台灣地名）

9. [1]be [3]fond [1]of（phr.）喜歡

　　【相關字彙】

　　[3]fond [fɑnd]（adj.）喜歡的；愛好的

10. [1]price [praɪs]（n.）①價格；價錢　②代價；犧牲　（phr.）①price index 物價指數　②price tag 價格標籤　③at any price 不惜任何代價　☆ [5]index（n.）指數　[3]tag（n.）標籤

11. [2]result [1]in（phr.）導致……的結果

12. autistic [ɔˋtɪstɪk]（adj.）自閉症的

　　【相關字彙】

　　autism [ˋɔtɪzəm]（n.）（心理）自閉症

13. [1]for [1]life（phr.）一生

14. [3]tulip [ˋtjuləp]（n.）鬱金香

15. [3]cherry [4]blossom（phr.）櫻花

　　【相關字彙】

　　[3]cherry [ˋtʃɛrɪ]（n.）①櫻桃　②櫻桃樹

　　[4]blossom [ˋblɑsəm]（n.）①花　②開花（期）

16. [4]bloom [blum]（n.）/（v.）①花　②開花（期）　（phr.）in （full）bloom 盛開

17. ³occasion [ə`keʒən]（n.）①場合；時刻；重大活動 ②機會；時機 ③理由 （phr.）①on occasion 偶爾；有時 ②have（no）occasion to（沒）有做⋯⋯的理由（必要）③give occasion to 引起；使發生 （v.）導致；引起

18. ¹next-¹door [`nɛkst͵dor]（adj.）隔壁的

19. ¹decide ¹to（phr.）決定去做

20. ¹make ¹a ¹deal（phr.）約定
    【相關字彙】
    ¹deal [dil]（v.）①對付；處理；對待 ②買賣；經營 ③分配 （n.）①數量 ②交易
    ³dealer [`dilɚ]（n.）商人

21. ²winner [`wɪnɚ]（n.）勝利者
    【相關字彙與重要片語】
    ¹win [wɪn]（v.）獲勝；贏得 （phr.）①win out/through 擺脫困境；終獲成功 ②win Sb.'s heart 贏得某人的愛

22. ⁶beverage [`bɛvərɪdʒ]（n.）飲料

23. ¹paper, ²scissors, ¹stone（phr.）（遊戲）剪刀；石頭；布
    【諺】Kill two birds with one stone. 一石二鳥。
    【諺】A rolling stone gathers no moss. 滾石不生苔。
        rolling（adj.）滾動的 ²gather（v.）積聚
        ⁵moss（n.）苔蘚

24. ¹shout [ʃaut]（v.）呼喊；喊叫 （phr.）shout at 對⋯⋯大叫

25. ²stick ¹to（phr.）①黏住 ②堅持

【相關字彙與重要片語】

²stick [stɪk]（n.）棍棒；手杖　（v.）①刺；戳　②黏著；釘住　③堅持　（phr.）①stick at 堅持做　②（口）stick it out堅持到底

26. ⁶aboriginal [ˌæbəˈrɪdʒənl]（adj.）土著（居民）的；原始的　（n.）原住民

27. ⁶cemetery [ˈsɛməˌtɛrɪ]（n.）墓地；公墓

28. ²pattern [ˈpætən]（n.）①模範；榜樣　②圖案；圖形　③類型；型式

29. totem [ˈtotəm]（n.）圖騰（像）

30. tattoo [tæˈtu]（n.）／（v.）刺青

31. ⁶exotic [ɛgˈzɑtɪk]（adj.）①異國情調的　②外來的；外國產的　（n.）舶來品

32. ³feather [ˈfɛðə]（n.）羽毛　（phr.）as light as a feather 輕如鴻毛

【諺】Birds of a feather flock together. 物以類聚。

　　³flock（v.）聚集

【諺】Fine feathers make fine birds. 佛靠金裝，人靠衣裝。

33. ¹rub Sb. ¹the ¹wrong ¹way（phr.）惹惱某人

【相關字彙】

¹rub [rʌb]（v.）①擦；揉　②摩擦

¹rubber [ˈrʌbə]（n.）①橡膠　②橡皮筋

34. ¹continue [kənˈtɪnjʊ]（v.）繼續

35. unlucky [ʌnˈlʌkɪ]（adj.）①不幸的 ②<u>不吉利的</u>

【相關字彙與重要片語】

¹lucky [ˈlʌkɪ]（adj.）幸運的 （phr.）Lucky you/me！ 你/我真走運！

²luck [lʌk]（n.）運氣；幸運 （phr.）①be in/out of luck 好/壞 運的 ②down on one's luck 倒楣；不走運地 ③Good luck（to you）！祝你好運！

36. ³warn [wɔrn]（v.）①警告 ②通知 （phr.）①warn away/off 警告不得靠近 ②warn Sb. not to do 警告人不要做

37. ³pause [pɔz]（v.）/（n.）中斷；暫停 （phr.）in/at pause 中止；暫停

38. ¹carry ¹on ¹with（phr.）繼續

【相關字彙】

¹carry [ˈkærɪ]（v.）①（用手、肩等）挑；抱；背；提；扛；搬 ②搬運 ③攜帶

39. ⁴competition [ˌkɑmpəˈtɪʃən]（n.）競爭；比賽

【相關字彙與重要片語】

³compete [kəmˈpit]（v.）競爭；匹敵 （phr.）①compete against 競爭 ②compete with 與……競爭

⁴competitive [kəmˈpɛtətɪv]（adj.）競爭性的

⁴competitor [kəmˈpɛtətɚ]（n.）競爭者；對手；敵手

40. ³stuff [stʌf]（n.）①材料；原料 ②<u>事情</u>；物品 （v.）填塞 （phr.）stuff into 把……塞進

41. ⁵chatter [`tʃætɚ] (v.) / (n.) ①喋喋不休地說 ②鳥囀聲 ③潺潺流水聲

42. ¹on ¹and ¹on (phr.) 繼續不停地

43. ⁴circular [`sɝkjəlɚ] (adj.) ①圓形的 ②循環的

【相關字彙與重要片語】

²circle [`sɝkḷ] (n.) ①圓；圓形 ②循環 (phr.) ①go round in circles 在原地兜圈子；毫無成效地瞎忙 ②have a large circle of friends 交遊廣泛

⁴circulate [`sɝkjəˌlet] (v.) ①流通；循環 ②使傳播 ③（貨幣）流通

⁴circulation [`sɝkjəˌleʃən] (n.) ①循環 ②（報刊）發行量 ③流通 (phr.) blood circulation 血液循環

44. ²extra [`ɛkstrə] (adj.) / (adv.) 額外的（地）；特別的（地） (n.) 額外（或特別的）東西

45. ⁵cautious [`kɔʃəs] (adj.) 極小心的；慎重的；謹慎的 (phr.) be cautious about/of/with 十分小心的；謹慎的

【相關字彙】

⁵caution [`kɔʃən] (n.) ①謹慎；小心 ②警戒 (v.) 警告

46. ⁴observation [ˌɑbzɝ`veʃən] (n.) 觀察；觀察力 (phr.) ①a man of observation 一位觀察力敏銳的人 ②under observation 被監視

【相關字彙】

³observe [əb`zɝv] (v.) ①觀察；注意 ②遵守

[5]observer [əbˋzɝvɚ]（n.）觀察家

47. [1]check [1]out（phr.）①檢查 ②結帳離開

【相關字彙與重要片語】

[1]check [tʃɛk]（v.）①阻止；遏止 ②檢查；查看 （n.）①支票 ②帳單 （phr.）draw a check 開支票

☆ [1]draw（v.）開支票

[5]checkbook [ˋtʃɛkˏbʊk]（n.）支票簿

[5]check-in [ˋtʃɛkˏɪn]（n.）投宿；登記

48. [1]in [1]fact（phr.）事實上

【相關字彙】

[1]fact [fækt]（n.）事實；真相

49. unnamed [ʌnˋnemd]（adj.）未命名的

50. [1]it [1]is [1]time [1]for（phr.）該是……時候了

51. sunset [ˋsʌnˏsɛt]（n.）夕陽（的景象）

52. [3]cricket [ˋkrɪkɪt]（n.）①蟋蟀 ②板球

53. [1]along [1]with（phr.）連同一起

54. [5]howl [haʊl]（v.）①（狼）嗥叫 ②（風）呼嘯 ③嚎啕大哭 （n.）嚎啕大哭

55. [6]bleak [blik]（adj.）①寒冷刺骨的 ②荒涼的

56. [1]kick [1]up [1]a [5]fuss（phr.）起鬨

【相關字彙與重要片語】

[1]kick [kɪk]（v.）/（n.）踢 （phr.）kick out 解僱

[5]fuss [fʌs]（n.）大驚小怪 （phr.）make a fuss 大驚小怪

57. ¹get ¹on ¹with（phr.）繼續做

58. ³determine [dɪˈtɜmɪn]（v.）①決定；下決心 ②確定
　　【相關字彙】
　　⁴determination [dɪˌtɜməˈneʃən]（n.）①決心 ②確定

59. ²fail ¹to（phr.）失敗；未能
　　【相關字彙】
　　²fail [fel]（v.）①失敗 ②不及格 ③衰退
　　²failure [ˈfeljə]（n.）①失敗 ②失敗者；失敗的事 ③不足；
　　缺乏

60. ¹round [raʊnd]（adj.）①圓的 ②肥胖的；豐滿的 （n.）一
　　回合；一輪 （v.）①變圓 ②環繞
　　【諺】Love makes the world go round. 愛使世界運轉。

61. ¹under ¹the ¹weather（phr.）（情緒或身體上）不舒服

62. ¹turn ¹around（phr.）轉身

63. ¹keep ¹an ¹eye ¹on（phr.）特別注意

64. ¹make one's ¹blood ¹run ¹cold（phr.）令人毛骨悚然

65. ³farther [ˈfɑrðə]（adv.）/（adj.）（距離或時間）更遠；進
　　一步

66. ⁴identify [aɪˈdɛntəˌfaɪ]（v.）①辨識；認出 ②視……為同一事
　　物 （phr.）identify with 認同；感同身受
　　【相關字彙】
　　³identity [aɪˈdɛntətɪ]（n.）①同一；一致 ②身分

67. shadowy [ˈʃædəwɪ]（adj.）①幽暗的 ②朦朧的 ③幽靈般的

68. ²monster [ˈmɑnstɚ]（n.）怪物；怪獸

69. ¹be adjacent ¹to（phr.）毗連；鄰近

70. ⁵cling ¹to（phr.）緊握不放；緊抓
    【相關字彙】
    ⁵cling [klɪŋ]（v.）①黏住；緊握不放 ②執著

71. ⁴backpack [ˈbækˌpæk]（n.）（登山、遠足用的）背包

72. ³somewhat [ˈsʌmˌhwɑt]（adv.）有點；稍微

73. ²bloody [ˈblʌdɪ]（adj.）①血淋淋；流血的 ②嗜殺的；殘忍的

74. hideous [ˈhɪdɪəs]（adj.）極醜陋的

75. distorted [dɪsˈtɔrtɪd]（adj.）扭曲的
    【相關字彙】
    ⁶distort [dɪsˈtɔrt]（v.）①扭曲 ②歪曲；曲解

76. ¹wear [wɛr]（v.）①穿；佩帶 ②面露；面帶 ③磨損；穿破
    （n.）衣服 （phr.）wear St./Sb. out 磨損某事物/使某人
    疲乏

77. ⁶symbolic [sɪmˈbɑlɪk]（adj.）象徵的
    【相關字彙】
    ²symbol [ˈsɪmbl̩]（n.）①象徵 ②符號；記號
    ⁶symbolize [ˈsɪmbl̩ˌaɪz]（v.）象徵

78. ⁴decoration [ˌdɛkəˈreʃən]（n.）①裝飾（品）②勳章
    【相關字彙與重要片語】
    ²decorate [ˈdɛkəˌret]（v.）裝飾 （phr.）decorate with 用……
    裝飾

79. ²childlike [`tʃaɪldˌlaɪk] (adj.) 孩子般的

～ 第八章 ～
看電影

有一個關於在美國洛杉磯，一名警官大衛的故事。有一天，他在休假中，並沒有任何特別的事情去做。帶著空虛的（³vacant）心靈，他決定到外面放鬆（³relax）一下。他在郊外（³suburb）四處高興（¹joy）駕著車子兜風後，感到有一些兒疲勞的（⁵weary）而幾次打呵欠（²yawn）。天氣很熱。他把臉上的汗擦拭去。突然，他看見這條道路上陌生的（unfamiliar）轉角，一些巨大的（¹huge）樹旁，一間電影院吸引住他了。「這間戲院是何時在這兒營業的呢？」他感到疑惑著。可是，不知打哪兒來未知的事物，像是強大的（²powerful）魔力（²magic），在他身上起作用著。他於是深深地被引誘去進入這間戲院（⁴cinema）。因此，他將車子在停車場停好，並很快速地步行到這間戲院前面的大門口（²gate）。

∽ Chapter 8 ∾
Seeing Movies

There is a story about David who was a police officer in [1]Los Angeles, USA. One day, he was [2]on holiday and [3]had nothing in particular to do. With his [4]vacant mind, he decided to go outside to [5]relax for a while. After he [6]went for a [7]joy ride in his car around the [8]suburbs, he felt [9]a little [10]weary and [11]yawned several times. It was very hot. He [12]wiped the sweat off his face. Suddenly, he saw a [13]movie theater, next to some [14]huge trees [15]on an [16]unfamiliar corner of the road, which [17]appealed to him. "When did this theater [18]open up here?" he wondered. But something unknown from some place, like [19]powerful [20]magic, [21]took effect on him. He was then deeply [22]tempted to enter the [23]cinema. So, he parked his car in the [24]parking lot and went to the front [25]gate of this theater [26]on foot quickly.

　　稍後，他眼睛一瞥看到電影小手冊（⁶brochure），與印（¹print）在海報（³poster）上有關最新電影商業的（³commercial）廣告（³ad）。海報被固定於室外的電影院牆上。並且，他發現到：「噢！這間戲院，正放映我最近（⁴lately）一直有興趣的一部電影（²film）吧！」他幾天前已經看過從電影評論家（⁴critic）那裡，關於那部電影多種不同的（mixed）評論（²review）；但是，他想無論如何（²anyway），它會是一部好電影。此外，關於這部電影的口碑基本上（basically）也是令人滿意的（³satisfactory）。就在這一段時間裡，他確定看定這部電影了，並且馬上在前門的售票處買了一張電影票（¹ticket）。

　　這部大衛所選擇（²choose）電影的名稱（²title），叫做是《加州（California）連續（serial）瘋狂殺人魔（killer）》。整體（⁵overall）而言，影片中呈現（²present）許多連續的（consecutive）、不寒而慄的（horrifying），關於人們被無

Later on, he ^{27}took a glance at the movie ^{28}brochures and ^{29}commercial ^{30}ads about the newest movies ^{31}printed on the ^{32}posters. The posters were ^{33}fixed to the cinema walls outside. And he found out, "Oh! This theater is showing a ^{34}film which I have been interested in ^{35}lately!" He had checked the ^{36}mixed ^{37}reviews from ^{38}critics about that movie before several days, but he thought it would be a good movie ^{39}anyway. Besides, the ^{40}word of mouth about the movie was ^{41}basically ^{42}satisfactory ^{43}as well. ^{44}In the meantime, he was ^{45}sure to see the film and immediately bought a ^{46}ticket at the ^{47}box office at the front door.

The ^{48}title of the film which David ^{49}chose to see was called *Crazy* ^{50}*California* ^{51}*Serial* ^{52}*Killer*. ^{53}Overall, the film ^{54}presented many ^{55}consecutive scary scenes about people who were killed ^{56}ruthlessly. Nobody could escape when caught by the cold

情地（ruthlessly）謀殺（³murder）的片段。當被殺手抓住時，沒有人能安全地逃脫。但是，一件奇怪的、不合理之事是：每當電影播放那些駭人的殺人片段時，舞台（²stage）下的觀眾（³audience）卻是全然地哈哈大笑，毫無任何同情心（⁴sympathy）的樣子。

現在，電影又放映了一名年輕、像大美人的（⁵gorgeous）女子，由於她無止盡的虛榮心（⁵vanity）與慾望（²desire），而將要被變態的（morbid）兇手（⁴murderer）殘忍地（brutally）殺害可怕的片段。兇手先是在身體上虐待（⁶abuse）了她。因為恐懼，她突然大聲地嚎啕大哭（⁵wail）。一會兒過後，他試著從地板上清理（⁶cleanse）著她的血液。在那一刻，大衛不禁發了瘋一樣，而如此害怕的以至於他大聲尖叫著：「真是太可怕了啊！救命啊！」同一時間，所有觀眾中的每一人都轉向他笑著；然後，瞪著他看。但是，在廣闊的（⁴vast）黑暗之中，他們原來人類的臉孔竟然全都漸漸地消失（³vanish）了；卻變成

killer. But one weird thing that did not [57]make sense was: whenever the movie showed those [58]horrifying [59]murder scenes, the [60]audience away from the [61]stage laughed very loudly, without having any [62]sympathy at all.

Now, the film also showed a horrible scene of a young, [63]gorgeous lady who was going to be killed [64]brutally by the [65]morbid [66]murderer because of her endless [67]vanity and [68]desire. The killer [69]abused her physically first. She [70]burst into loud [71]wails because of fear. After a while, he tried to [72]cleanse her blood from the floor. At that point, David could not help [73]losing his head and was so scared that he screamed loudly. "It is too scary! Help!" At the same time, everyone in the audience turned to him, smiled, and then [74]stared at him. But in [75]vast darkness, [76]instead of the audience's faces around him

了一個接著一個白色的骷髏頭（⁵skull），而不是在電影院中環繞著他的觀眾臉孔。此外，在那一刻裡，他發覺到非常令人害怕的（terrifying）骷髏頭正面向著他，並且似乎是（seemingly）顯露出他們對他毫無幽默感，帶著十分憎恨（⁴hatred）的表情（¹look）。對他們而言，殺人是一件多麼有趣的事啊！

in the theater, their human faces all actually gradually [77]vanished and became the white [78]skulls [79]one by one. Moreover, at that moment, he realized that there were very [80]terrifying skulls facing him and [81]seemingly showing their [82]looks with a lot of [83]hatred to him for his not having [84]a sense of humor at all. To them, how interesting it was to murder people!

Chapter 8

Vocabulary

1. Los Angeles 洛杉磯（美國城市名）

2. ¹on ¹holiday（phr.）在休假中

3. ¹have ¹nothing ¹in ²particular ¹to ¹do（phr.）沒什麼特別要做的事

4. ³vacant [`vekənt]（adj.）①空的；空白的 ②（心靈）空虛的
   【相關字彙】
   ⁵vacancy [`vekənsı]（n.）①空虛 ②空閒 ③空缺

5. ³relax [rı`læks]（v.）①鬆懈；鬆弛 ②使輕鬆；放輕鬆
   【相關字彙】
   ⁴relaxation [ˌrilæk`seʃən]（n.）放鬆；輕鬆

6. ¹go ¹for ¹a ¹ride（phr.）（騎/開車）兜風；騎馬出遊

7. ¹joy [dʒɔɪ]（n.）歡樂；高興

8. ³suburb [`sʌbɝb]（n.）市郊；郊外
   【相關字彙】
   ⁶suburban [sə`bɝbən]（adj.）郊外的

9. ¹a ¹little（phr.）一些；一點
   【諺】Many a little makes a mickle. 積少成多。
        mickle（n.）大；多
   【諺】A little neglect may breed great mischief.

星星之火可以燎原。　⁴neglect（v.）忽略

⁴breed（v.）產生

10. ⁵weary [ˈwɪrɪ]（adj.）①疲勞的　②厭倦的　（v.）使疲倦；使
厭倦　（phr.）weary out 使筋疲力竭

11. ²yawn [jɔn]（v.）/（n.）（打）呵欠

12. ³wipe ¹off（phr.）擦掉
【相關字彙】
³wipe [waɪp]（v.）擦拭；擦掉

13. ¹movie ²theater（phr.）電影院
【相關字彙】
²theater [ˈθɪətɚ]（n.）劇場；電影院

14. ¹huge [hjudʒ]（adj.）巨大的

15. ¹on ¹a ²corner ¹of（phr.）在……的轉角

16. unfamiliar [ˌʌnfəˈmɪljɚ]（adj.）陌生的；不熟悉的
【相關字彙】
³familiar [fəˈmɪljɚ]（adj.）①親密的；親近的　②通曉的　③
熟悉的；世所周知的
⁶familiarity [fəˌmɪlɪˈærətɪ]（n.）熟悉；親近

17. ³appeal ¹to（phr.）吸引
【相關字彙與重要片語】
³appeal [əˈpil]（v.）①懇求；懇請　②訴諸　③有吸引力
（n.）①懇求；懇請　②（法律）上訴　③魅力　（phr.）
①appeal for 請求　②lodge/enter an appeal 提出上訴

☆ ⁵lodge（v.）提出

18．¹open ¹up（phr.）開張；開門營業

19．²powerful [ˋpaʊəfəl]（adj.）強大的

【相關字彙與重要片語】

¹power [ˋpaʊə]（n.）①權力 ②力量 （phr.）①come to/ into power 當權；開始執政 ②beyond/out of/not within one's power 超越某人能力所及

【諺】Knowledge is <u>power</u>. 知識就是力量。

20．²magic [ˋmædʒɪk]（n.）①魔法；魔術 ②<u>魔力；不可思議的 力量</u> （adj.）①魔法的 ②有魔力的；不可思議的 （phr.）①magic wand 魔杖 ②magic bullet（俚）仙丹妙藥 ③magic square 魔術方塊 ☆ wand（n.）棒杖 ³bullet（n.）子彈 ²square（n.）正方形；方塊；廣場

【相關字彙】

²magician [məˋdʒɪʃən]（n.）魔術師

21．²take ²effect ¹on Sb.（phr.）在某人身上起了作用

22．¹be ⁵tempted ¹to（phr.）被誘惑做

【相關字彙】

⁵tempt [tɛmpt]（v.）①刺激 ②誘惑

23．⁴cinema [ˋsɪnəmə]（n.）戲院；電影院

24．¹parking ¹lot（phr.）停車場

【相關字彙與重要片語】

¹lot [lɑt]（n.）①抽籤；籤 ②命運 ③很多 （phr.）draw

lots 抽籤 ☆ ¹draw（v.）抽（籤）

25. ²gate [get]（n.）①<u>大門</u>（口）②出入口；登機門

26. ¹on ¹foot（phr.）步行

27. ¹take ¹a ³glance ¹at（phr.）對……匆匆一看
【相關字彙】

³glance [glæns]（v.）/（n.）一瞥；掃視

28. ⁶brochure [broˋʃur]（n.）小冊子

29. ³commercial [kəˋmɝʃəl]（adj.）<u>商業的</u>（n.）（電視、廣播）商業廣告

30. ³advertisement/³ad [ˏædvɚˋtaɪzmənt] / [æd]（n.）廣告；宣傳

31. ¹print [prɪnt]（v.）①<u>印；印刷</u> ②出版 ③以印刷體書寫
（n.）①印刷；印刷字體 ②印痕；印記 ③（美）印刷品
（phr.）①out of print 已絕版 ②put into print 付印
【相關字彙】

²printer [ˋprɪntɚ]（n.）①印刷者 ②印刷業者 ③（電腦）印表機；印刷機

32. ³poster [ˋpostɚ]（n.）①<u>海報</u> ②廣告（畫）③佈告

33. ¹be ¹fixed ¹to（phr.）被固定在

34. ²film [fɪlm]（n.）①膠捲；軟片 ②<u>影片；電影</u> ③薄膜
（v.）把……拍成電影 （phr.）①shoot/take a film 拍攝影片 ②put a novel on the films 把小說搬上銀幕（或改編成電影）

35. ⁴lately [ˋletlɪ]（adv.）近來；最近

36. mixed [mɪkst]（adj）①混合的；混雜的 ②多種不同的（反應、回應、評論等）

【相關字彙與重要片語】

²mix [mɪks]（v.）①混合 ②混淆 ③給……配製

³mixture [ˋmɪkstʃɚ]（n.）混合物 （phr.）the mixture as before 換湯不換藥的東西

37. ²review [rɪˋvju]（n.）/（v.）①復習 ②批評；評論 ③再檢查

38. ⁴critic [ˋkrɪtɪk]（n.）批評家；評論家

【相關字彙與重要片語】

⁴critical [ˋkrɪtɪk!]（adj.）①批評的；評論的 ②吹毛求疵的 ③危急的；關鍵性的 （phr.）be in a critical condition 情況危急

⁴criticize [ˋkrɪtə͵saɪz]（v.）①批評；評論 ②苛求；挑剔

⁴criticism [ˋkrɪtə͵sɪzəm]（n.）①批評，評論 ②苛求；挑剔 （phr.）constructive criticism 建設性的評論

☆ ⁴constructive（adj.）結構的

39. ²anyway [ˋɛnɪ͵we]（adv.）無論如何

40. ¹word ¹of ¹mouth（phr.）口碑

41. basically [ˋbesɪk!ɪ]（adv.）在根本上

【相關字彙與重要片語】

¹basic [ˋbesɪk]（adj.）①根本的,基礎的 ②基礎 （phr.）basic training（新兵的）基本訓練 ☆ ¹train（v.）訓練

²basics [ˋbesɪks]（n.）①基礎 ②基本原理；基本原則

²basis [ˋbesɪs]（n.）基礎；根據 （phr.）on the basis of 基於

42. ³satisfactory [ˌsætɪsˋfæktərɪ]（adj.）令人滿意的；符合要求的

43. ¹as ¹well（phr.）也

44. ¹in ¹the ⁵meantime（phr.）在……期間；同時

【相關字彙】

⁵meantime [ˋminˌtaɪm]（n.）其間；同時

45. ¹be ¹sure ¹to ¹do St.（phr.）一定要去做某事

46. ¹ticket [ˋtɪkɪt]（n.）票；入場券 （phr.）①an advance ticket 預售票 ②a one-way/round-trip ticket（美）單程/來回 票 ③admission by ticket（告示語）憑票入場

☆ ⁴admission （n.）入場卷；進入許可

47. ¹box ¹office（phr.）售票處

48. ²title [ˋtaɪtl]（n.）①標題；名稱 ②頭銜；稱號 （v.）①加標題於 ②授頭銜於

49. ²choose [tʃuz]（v.）選擇 （phr.）cannot choose but 只得

【相關字彙與重要片語】

²choice [tʃɔɪs]（n.）選擇 （phr.）①make choice of 選定 ②have no choice but to do 不得不做 ③at one's own choice 隨意

50. California [ˌkæləˋfɔrnjə] 加州（美國州名）

51. serial [ˋsɪrɪəl]（adj.）①連續的 ②連載的 （n.）連載小說；

定期刊物；連續劇

52. killer [ˈkɪlɚ]（n.）殺手

53. ⁵overall [ˈovɚˌɔl]（adj.）整體的；全部的　（n.）工作服；防護服

　　　　* [ˌovɚˈɔl]（adv.）整體；全部

54. ²present [prɪˈzɛnt]（v.）呈現

　　　　* [ˈprɛznt]（adj.）①出席的　②現在的　（n.）①現在；目前　②禮物

【相關字彙】

²presence [ˈprɛzns]（n.）①出席；在場　②面前；眼前

⁴presentation [ˌprizɛnˈteʃən]（n.）①贈送　②上演　③呈現

55. consecutive [kənˈsɛkjutɪv]（adj.）連續的

56. ruthlessly [ˈruθlɪslɪ]（adv.）冷酷地；無情地

57. ¹make ¹sense（phr.）合理；有道理

【相關字彙與重要片語】

¹sense [sɛns]（n.）①感覺；感官　②意識　③意義；意思　（v.）感覺到；意識到　（phr.）①make sense of 理解　②come to one's senses 甦醒過來；清醒　③the moral sense 道德觀念

³sensible [ˈsɛnsəbl]（adj.）①意識到的　②有知覺的　③可注意到的

58. horrifying [ˈhɔrəfaɪɪŋ]（adj.）令人恐懼的；不寒而慄的

【相關字彙】

⁴horrify [ˈhɔrəˌfaɪ]（v.）使恐懼；使驚懼

59. ³murder [ˈmɝdɚ]（v.）謀殺；殺死 （n.）謀殺（案）
（phr.）murder in the first degree（美）（法律）第一級謀
殺

☆ ²degree（n.）程度；等級

【諺】Murder will out. 若要人不知，除非己莫爲。

60. ³audience [ˈɔdɪəns]（n.）①聽眾；觀眾 ②聽；傾聽 （phr.）
①give audience to 聽取；接見；召見 ②have audience of/have
an audience with 拜會；拜謁

61. ²stage [stedʒ]（v.）演出；上演 （n.）①舞台 ②階段；時期
（phr.）①bring on/to the stage 上演 ②make stage a comeback
東山再起 ③go on the stage 當演員

62. ⁴sympathy [ˈsɪmpəθɪ]（n.）同情（心）；憐憫
【相關字彙與重要片語】
⁴sympathetic [ˌsɪmpəˈθɛtɪk]（adj.）①有同情心的 ②同感
的；贊成的
⁵sympathize [ˈsɪmpəˌθaɪz]（v.）①同情 ②同感；同意
（phr.）sympathize with Sb. 同情某人

63. ⁵gorgeous [ˈgɔrdʒəs]（adj.）①非常漂亮的；像大美人的 ②
豪華的；絢爛的；華麗的

64. brutally [ˈbrutḷɪ]（adv.）殘忍地
【相關字彙】
⁴brutal [ˈbrutḷ]（adj.）①殘忍的 ②嚴苛的

⁶brute ［brut］（n.）①人面獸心的人　②獸；畜生　（adj.）①畜生　②殘忍的

65. morbid ［`mɔrbɪd］（adj.）變態的；病態的

66. ⁴murderer ［`mɝdərə］（n.）兇手

67. ⁵vanity ［`vænətɪ］（n.）①空虛；空幻　②虛榮（心）③無用；無價值　（phr.）minister to vanity 滿足虛榮心

☆ ⁴minister（v.）伺候；盡力

【相關字彙與重要片語】

⁴vain ［ven］（adj.）①徒然的；無效的　②自負的；虛榮心強的　（phr.）in vain 徒勞；無結果的

68. ²desire ［dɪ`zaɪr］（n.）/（v.）願望；意欲；希冀　（phr.）have a desire for 渴望

69. ⁶abuse ［ə`bjus］（v.）①濫用；妄用　②虐待；凌虐　③辱罵　（phr.）①an abuse of power 濫用權力　②personal abuse 人身攻擊

70. ²burst ¹into（phr.）突然發出

【相關字彙與重要片語】

²burst ［bɝst］（v.）/（n.）①爆炸；破裂　②爆發；突發　（phr.）burst out 突然……起來

71. ⁵wail ［wel］（v.）①嚎啕大哭；哀泣　②（風等）呼嘯；（警笛等）尖嘯　（n.）①慟哭聲　②呼嘯聲；尖嘯聲

72. ⁶cleanse ［klɛnz］（v.）①使清潔；清理　②使純潔；使純淨　（phr.）cleanse the soul/heart of sin 淨滌心靈

73. ^{1}lose one's ^{1}head（phr.）失去理智

74. ^{3}stare ^{1}at（phr.）盯；凝視

【相關字彙】

^{3}stare ［stɛr］（v.）／（n.）盯；凝視

75. ^{4}vast ［væst］（adj.）廣大的；廣闊的

76. ^{3}instead ^{1}of（phr.）代替；而不是

77. ^{3}vanish ［ˋvænɪʃ］（v.）消失；消散

78. ^{5}skull ［skʌl］（n.）①骷髏頭；頭骨 ②（象徵死亡的）骷髏畫 ③腦袋 （phr.）have a thick skull 笨頭笨腦

☆ ^{2}thick（adj.）（口）笨的

79. ^{1}one ^{1}by ^{1}one（phr.）一個接 ·個

80. terrifying ［ˋtɛrəfaɪɪŋ］（adj.）令人害怕的

【相關字彙與重要片語】

^{4}terrify ［ˋtɛrəˌfaɪ］（v.）使害怕；使恐怖 （phr.）①terrify Sb. into doing 威脅某人做某事 ②be terrified at/with 被……嚇一跳

^{4}terror ［ˋtɛrɚ］（n.）恐怖；使人會怕的人（或事物）（phr.）①be a terror to 使……恐怖的人（或事物） ②strike terror into one's heart 使人膽戰心驚

☆ ^{2}strike（v.）使穿透；攻擊

81. seemingly ［ˋsimɪŋlɪ］（adv.）表面上；似乎是

82. ^{1}look ［lʊk］（n.）臉色；表情

【諺】Look before you leap. 三思而後行。

^{3}leap（v.）跳

83．^{4}hatred［`hetrɪd］（n.）憎恨 （phr.）①harbor hatred 心懷仇恨 ②a legacy of hatred 世仇；宿仇 ③sow the seeds of hatred 撒下仇恨的種子

☆ ^{3}harbor（v.）心懷 ^{1}legacy（n.）遺產；留給後人的東西 ^{5}sow（v.）播種 ^{1}seed （n.）種子

84．^{1}a ^{1}sense ^{1}of ^{2}humor（phr.）幽默感

【相關字彙與重要片語】

^{2}humor［`hjumɚ］（n.）幽默；滑稽 （phr.）in the/no humor for 有興致/沒心思

^{3}humorous［`hjumərəs］（adj.）幽默的；滑稽的

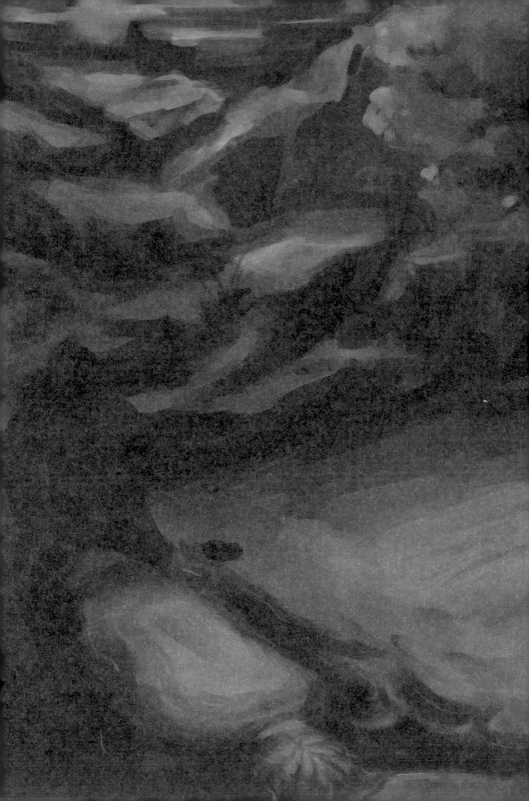

～ 第九章 ～
真相

意外總是發生在溪流（²stream）之中。大約是在三年前，小軍與小彬是兩位非常要好的朋友。有一天，天氣很熱。他們相約一起去游泳。他們騎著他們的交通工具（³vehicle），到台灣的花蓮縣郊外碰頭。在那裡人們可見到那些美麗的溪谷（²valley）、野生生物（⁵wildlife）、山脈和溫泉……等等。無疑地，到處都是值得的（⁵worthwhile），讓觀光客（³tourist）們能遊覽（¹visit）與探索（⁴explore）一番。然而，因為兩者之中無一（³neither）很擅長於游泳；不幸地，不久後兩人遭遇到一條溪中些許急（²rapid）流。小軍立即緊緊抓牢（⁵clutch）他身旁溪中的大石塊不放；但是，小彬卻突然抽筋（⁶cramp）了。接著，小彬被水沖走了，並且被深的小溪（³brook）中的眾多暗流（undercurrent）吞沒了。很遺憾地，小彬並沒有脫離危險（¹danger）。稍後，他的身體再次浮出

∼ Chapter 9 ∼
The Truth

Accidents always happen in [1]streams. Xiao–jun and Xiao–bing were two very good friends about three years ago. One day, the weather was very hot. They [2]planned to go swimming together. They rode their [3]vehicles to meet [4]on the outskirts of [5]Hualien County, Taiwan, where people could see those beautiful [6]valleys, [7]wildlife, mountains, [8]hot springs [9]and so on. It was surely [10]worthwhile for [11]tourists to [12]visit and [13]explore everywhere. However, because [14]neither of them was very [15]good at swimming, unfortunately, [16]before long, the two people underwent some very [17]rapid currents in one stream. Immediately, Xiao–jun [18]clutched a huge rock beside him in the stream, but Xiao–bing was suddenly [19]seized with a [20]cramp. Then, Xiao–bing was [21]swept away by the water and [22]swallowed （resurface）來而被小軍發現後，小彬無可避免地（inevitably）變得是一具冰冷、沒有體溫（³warmth）的屍體了。

　　由於時間已晚，而且這件意外亦是以難以預料的（unforeseen）方式發生了，身為小彬的好朋友，小軍，在沒有很多心理上地（psychologically）準備之下；卻只是害怕地逃跑了。他自己也受了傷，而必須留下他朋友的屍體在岸邊。由於他朋友的死亡，目前的小軍誠然是非常悲傷與害怕的。因為對於荒郊野外的路線（⁴route）並不熟悉，對他來說要找到正確的路回家並不容易。最後，他迷路了。這時，終日的行走使得可憐的小軍筋疲力竭。因此，為了保險起見，他心想必須找一處能渡過今晚。他四處看看；接著，他看到靠近下游的（downstream）河床（riverbed）的一棟建築物（¹building）廢墟（⁴ruins）。他敲了幾次門之後，而沒人應門，他發現到門並沒

up by many ²³undercurrents deep in the ²⁴brook. ²⁵It was a pity that Xiao-bing could not escape ²⁶danger. Later, after his body ²⁷resurfaced and was discovered by Xiao-jun, Xiao-bing ²⁸inevitably became a cold corpse with no ²⁹warmth.

³⁰Owing to the late time, and also the ³¹unforeseen ways in which the accident had happened, as a good friend of Xiao-bing, Xiao-Jun, without being ³²psychologically prepared, simply fled in fear. He also got hurt himself and had to leave his friend's body ³³on the shore. To be sure, Xiao-jun was very sad and scared now because of his friend's death. It was not easy for him to find the right way home because he was not ³⁴familiar with the ³⁵route in the wilderness. Finally, he was lost. At this point, poor Xiao-jun was ³⁶exhausted from walking ³⁷all day long. Thus, ³⁸to be on the safe side, he thought that he needed to find a place to ³⁹spend the night. He looked

有鎖。似乎這棟陳舊的建築物被遺棄了很多年了。他決定待在那個地方一晚，並內心盼望著隔天，在天破曉（²dawn）後，能夠找到回家的路。

　　直到深夜時，小軍好像透過窗戶聽到有人躲在灌木叢（³bush）中，和傳出有人輕輕的腳步聲（footstep）。事情更糟糕的是，小彬哀傷的哭泣聲竟然充滿在小軍那晚住的地方。悲痛（⁴grief）萬分的小軍，住在這棟建築物裡變得更加地害怕了。而且，他一直做著惡夢。當然，他也沒睡得很好。他持續不斷地夢見死去的小彬回來找尋他，意圖著糾纏（⁵haunt）著他，並且不讓他離開。

around, and then he saw the [40]ruins of a [41]building near the [42]riverbed [43]downstream. After he knocked at the door a couple of times and nobody answered, he found it was unlocked. It seemed that the old building had been deserted for many years. He decided to stay at that place for one night and [44]yearned for his way home after [45]dawn the next day.

[46]Deep into the night, Xiao-jun seemed to hear through the windows that someone had hidden in the [47]bushes, and there came the gentle sound of people's [48]footsteps. [49]To make matters worse, it was the sound of Xiao-bing's sad crying that actually filled the area Xiao-jun occupied that night. Xiao-jun, with much [50]grief, became even more scared while living inside the building, and he kept having nightmares. Of course, he did not sleep very well, either. He kept dreaming that dead Xiao-bing came to [51]look for him. The ghost [52]intended to [53]haunt him and did not let him leave.

　　突然，小軍從外面聽到有什麼東西，一位幽靈似的（ghostly）人影正在呼喚著他，戲弄（³tease）著他說：「小軍，我好冷！哦！我也好孤單呀！請趕快來陪伴（⁴accompany）我吧！我們不是最要好的朋友嗎？你很膽小（¹chicken）耶！你忘記了我們所共有（²share）兄弟情誼（⁵brotherhood）嗎？」現在小軍待在室內（³indoors），看到外面站著一個黑影，驚嚇到魂不附體了。就在那時，小軍發覺自己再也無法容忍（⁴tolerate）一丁點兒，來自於他朋友鬼魂口頭的（⁵verbal）威脅（³threat）。他想要勇敢地（valiantly）對鬼做出報復。但是，實際上，對於他處理這種情況，最佳的策略（³strategy）就是打開門而拔腿一跑。當他開始跑時，小軍在空氣中聽見了有什麼東西，空氣中，事實上回響著來自鬼魂的一個顫抖的（trembling）聲音。鬼說道：「你看見你的身體了嗎？你確定你現在還活著嗎？」當聽見鬼對他所說的話，小軍往下一看他的身體；他卻驚恐地看到了一件事實。當他跑時，沒有腳，他自己的下半身竟然漂浮於地面之上，流著血。

Suddenly, Xiao-jun heard something from outside ; a [54]ghostly figure was calling and [55]teasing him. "Xiao-jun, I am so cold. Oh, I am very lonely, too! Please come to [56]accompany me quickly. Are we not best friends? You're [57]chicken! Have you [58]forgotten about the [59]brotherhood we [60]shared?" Now, Xiao-bing, staying [61]indoors, was scared to death to see a black shadow standing outside. Just then, Xiao-jun found that he could not [62]tolerate the least amount of [63]verbal [64]threats anymore from his friend's ghost. He wanted to [65]valiantly retaliate against the ghost. But actually, the best [66]strategy for him to [67]deal with the situation was just to open the door and [68]run away. When he started to run, Xiao-jun heard something in the air, and it, in fact, [69]echoed with a [70]trembling sound from the ghost. "Do you see your body? Are you sure that you are still alive now?" said the ghost. While listening to what the ghost said to him, Xiao-jun looked down at his body, but he was frightened to see the truth. Without feet, the lower parts of his body actually floated above the ground bleeding while running.

Chapter 9
Vocabulary

1. ²stream [strim]（n.）①溪；水流 ②趨勢；傾向 ③（光的）束；道 （v.）流動 （phr.）①the stream of times 時勢 ②go with the stream 順應潮流

2. ¹plan ¹to（phr.）計畫去做

3. ³vehicle [ˋviɪk!]（n.）①交通工具；車輛 ②媒介（物）

4. ¹on ¹the ⁵outskirts ¹of（phr.）在……郊外
   【相關字彙】
   ⁵outskirts [ˋaʊt.skɝts]（n.）郊外；市郊

5. Hualien ²County　花蓮縣（台灣地名）

6. ²valley [ˋvælɪ]（n.）①溪谷；峽谷 ②（河的）流域

7. ⁵wildlife [ˋwaɪld.laɪf]（n.）野生生物（總稱）

8. ¹hot ¹spring（phr.）溫泉

9. ¹and ¹so ¹on（phr.）等等

10. ⁵worthwhile [ˋwɝθˋhwaɪl]（adj.）①值得做的 ②值得花費時間（或金錢）的 ③有價值的
    【相關字彙與重要片語】
    ²worth [wɝθ]（adj.）/（n.）①有…的價值 ②值得
    ⁵worthy [ˋwɝðɪ]（adj.）①有價值的 ②值得的 （phr.）be worthy of 值得

11. ³tourist [ˈturɪst]（n.）觀光客

　　【相關字彙與重要片語】

　　²tour [tur]（n.）旅行；觀光 （phr.）①on tour 巡迴演出中

　　②go on a tour 去旅遊

　　³tourism [ˈturɪzəm]（n.）旅遊；觀光

12. ¹visit [ˈvɪzɪt]（v.）/（n.）①參觀；遊覽 ②拜訪；訪問 ③
　　逗留 （phr.）pay/make a visit to 訪問；參觀

　　【相關字彙】

　　²visitor [ˈvɪzɪtə]（n.）訪問者；觀光客

13. ⁴explore [ɪkˈsplor]（v.）探險；探索

　　【相關字彙】

　　explorer [ɪkˈsplorə]（n.）探險家

　　⁶exploration [ˌɛkspləˈreʃən]（n.）探險；探索；探測

14. ³neither [ˈniðə]（adj.）兩者皆非 （pron.）（兩者之中）無
　　一個 （adv.）也不

　　【諺】If you run after two hares, you will catch <u>neither</u>.

　　　　同時追兩兔，兩頭皆落空。

15. ¹be ¹good ¹at（phr.）精通

16. ¹before ¹long（phr.）不久

17. ²rapid [ˈræpɪd]（adj.）<u>快的；急促的</u> （n.）急流

18. ⁵clutch [klʌtʃ]（v.）緊緊抓牢

19. ¹be ³seized ¹with（phr.）突然感覺到或被侵擾

　　【相關字彙與重要片語】

^{3}seize ［siz］（v.）①抓住 ②（疾病等）侵襲 ③沒收；扣押
（phr.）seize on 把握

20. ^{6}cramp ［kræmp］（n.）①抽筋；<u>痙攣</u> ②鐵夾鉗；鐵箍
（v.）①抽筋；痙攣 ②約束；妨礙

21. ^{1}be ^{2}swept ^{1}away（phr.）①<u>沖走</u>；刮走 ②清除
【相關字彙與重要片語】
^{2}sweep ［swip］（v.）/（n.）①掃；清掃 ②（風等）刮起；
（浪等）沖走；席捲 ③掠過；擦過 （phr.）①at one/a
sweep 一下子 ②sweep off Sb. of his feet 使某人大爲讚賞或
折服
【諺】A new broom <u>sweeps</u> clean. 新官上任三把火。
^{3}broom（n.）掃帚

22. ^{1}be ^{2}swallowed ^{1}up（phr.）被吞沒
【相關字彙】
^{2}swallow ［`swɑlo］（v.）吞下；嚥下 （n.）燕子
【諺】One <u>swallow</u> does not make a summer. 勿以偏蓋全。

23. undercurrent ［`ʌndɚ‚kɝənt］（n.）暗流

24. ^{3}brook ［bruk］（n.）小溪；小河

25. ^{1}it ^{1}is ^{1}a ^{3}pity ^{1}that（phr.）很可惜的是；眞遺憾
【相關字彙與重要片語】
^{3}pity ［`pɪtɪ］（n.）/（v.）憐憫；同情 （phr.）①have/take
pity on 同情；憐憫 ②What a pity！多可惜；不幸
pitiful ［`pɪtɪfəl］（adj.）可憐的；令人同情的

26. ¹danger [`dendʒɚ] （n.）危險；危險的事物　（phr.）out of danger　脫離危險

27. resurface [ri`sɝfɪs] （v.）再次浮出；再次露出
    【相關字彙】
    ²surface [`sɝfɪs] （n.）表面；外觀；外表

28. inevitably [ɪn`ɛvətəblɪ] （adv.）必然地；不可避免地
    【相關字彙】
    ⁶inevitable [ɪn`ɛvətəbl̩] （adj.）必然的；不可避免的

29. ³warmth [wɔrmθ] （n.）①溫暖　②熱情　③<u>體溫</u>

30. owing ¹to（phr.）由於
    【相關字彙】
    owing [`oɪŋ] （adj.）欠著的；未付的
    ³owe [o] （v.）①欠債　②歸功於　③有盡……的義務

31. unforeseen [ʌnfor`sin] （adj.）未預見到的；難以預料的
    【相關字彙】
    ⁶foresee [for`si] （v.）預知；先覺

32. psychologically [saɪkə`lɑdʒɪklɪ] （adv.）心理（學）地
    【相關字彙】
    ⁴psychological [saɪkə`lɑdʒɪkl̩] （adj.）心理學的
    ⁴psychology [saɪ`kɑlədʒɪ] （n.）①心理學　②心理狀態

33. ¹on ¹the ¹shore（phr.）在岸邊

34. ¹be ³familiar ¹with（phr.）熟悉

35. ⁴route [rut] （n.）路線；航線

36. ⁴exhaust ¹from（phr.）使筋疲力竭

【相關字彙與重要片語】

⁴exhaust［ɪɡˋzɔst］（v.）①使疲憊 ②用完；耗盡 ③（氣體等）排放 （n.）（氣體等）排放 （phr.）auto exhausts 汽車排放廢氣 ☆ ³auto（n.）（美）（口）汽車

37. ¹all ¹day ¹long（phr.）終日

38. ¹to ¹be ¹on ¹the ¹safe ¹side（phr.）爲了保險起見

39. ¹spend ¹the ¹night（phr.）過夜

【相關字彙與重要片語】

¹spend［spɛnd］（v.）①花費 ②渡過 ③耗盡 （phr.）①spend one's breath/words 白費唇舌 ②spend money like water 揮金如土

40. ⁴ruin［ˋrʊɪn］（v.）①毀滅；毀壞 ②損害；傷害 （n.）①毀滅（的原因）；禍根 ②損害；傷害 ③廢墟；遺跡（常用複數） （phr.）①be the ruin of 成爲……毀滅的原因 ②draw ruin on oneself 導致自身的毀滅 ③bring to ruin 使沒落（或失敗）

41. ¹building［ˋbɪldɪŋ］（n.）建築物

【相關字彙與重要片語】

¹build［bɪld］（v.）①建築；建造 ②建立；增進 （phr.）①build up 增進；使增大 ②build a fire 生火 ③build on St. 在……基礎上發展

【諺】Rome was not built in a day.

羅馬不是一天所造成的。

42. riverbed [ˈrɪvɚˌbɛd]（n.）河床

43. downstream [ˈdaʊnˌstrim]（adj.）/（adv.）下游的（地）

44. [6]yearn [1]for（phr.）嚮往；渴望

【相關字彙】

[6]yearn [jɜn]（v.）嚮往；渴望

45. [2]dawn [dɔn]（n.）①黎明；破曉 ②開始；前兆 （v.）①破曉 ②醒悟 ③開始出現 （phr.）①dawn on 被理解 ②from dawn till / to dusk 從黎明到黃昏

☆ [5]dusk（n.）黃昏

46. [1]deep [1]into [1]the [1]night（phr.）直到深夜

47. [3]bush [bʊʃ]（n.）灌木（叢）

【諺】A bird in hand is worth two in the bush.
兩鳥在林，不如一鳥在手。

48. footstep [ˈfʊtˌstɛp]（n.）腳步（聲）

49. [1]to [1]make [1]matters [1]worse（phr.）更糟的是

【相關字彙與重要片語】

[1]matter [ˈmætɚ]（n.）①事情；問題 ②物質 ③毛病；麻煩事 （v.）認為……要緊 （phr.）①in the matter of 就……而論 ②make/be no matter 一點也無關緊要

【諺】No act of kindness, no matter how small, is ever wasted. 勿以善小而不為。

50. [4]grief [grif]（n.）悲傷；悲痛 （phr.）a heart big with grief

心中充滿悲哀

【相關字彙】

[4]grieve [griv] （v.）使悲傷

51. [1]look [1]for（phr.）找尋

52. [4]intend [1]to（phr.）打算

【相關字彙】

[4]intend [ɪnˋtɛnd]（v.）①打算 ②（爲……而）準備 ③意欲

53. [5]haunt [hɔnt]（v.）①常去（某處）；留連（某地）②糾纏（某人）③（幽靈等）出沒 （n.）①常出入之處 ②（動物等）棲息處

54. ghostly [ˋgostlɪ]（adj.）幽靈（似）的

55. [3]tease [tiz]（v.）①欺侮；戲弄 ②強求；纏擾 （n.）①戲弄取笑 ②愛戲弄人的人

56. [4]accompany [əˋkʌmpənɪ]（v.）①陪……同行；陪伴 ②伴奏 （phr.）①be accompanied by a friend 由朋友陪伴 ②the rain accompanied with wind 風雨交加

57. [1]chicken [ˋtʃɪkɪn]（n.）①雞；雛鳥 ②雞肉 ③（俚）膽小鬼 （adj.）（俚）膽怯的 （phr.）chicken and egg 難以決定因果關係的事

　　【諺】Don't count your chickens before they are hatched.

　　勿打如意算盤。 [3]hatch（v.）孵化

58. [1]forget [1]about（phr.）忘記

【相關字彙與重要片語】

¹forget [fəˋgɛt] (v.) 忘記；想不起 (phr.) forget it 算了；別放在心上

⁵forgetful [fəˋgɛtfəl] (adj.) 健忘的

59. ⁵brotherhood [ˋbrʌðəˏhud] (n.) 兄弟的關係；手足情誼

60. ²share [ʃɛr] (v.) ①分享；分擔 ②共有 ③股票；股份 (n.) (分擔) 的一部分 (phr.) ①share with 與……分享 ②go shares with Sb. in 和某人平分；共同分擔 ③a piece/slice/share of the pie (金錢、利潤等的) 一份；一杯羹

☆ ³slice (n.) 部分；份；片

61. ³indoors [ˋɪnˋdorz] (adv.) 在屋內；在室內

62. ⁴tolerate [ˋtɑləˏret] (v.) 忍受；忍耐；寬容

【相關字彙】

⁴tolerance [ˋtɑlərəns] (n.) 忍受

⁴tolerable [ˋtɑlərəbḷ] (adj.) 可忍受的

⁴tolerant [ˋtɑlərənt] (adj.) 忍受的；容忍的；寬恕的

63. ⁵verbal [ˋvɝbḷ] (adj.) ①文字上的；措辭的 ②口頭的 ③逐字的 (phr.) ①verbal/oral contract (法律) 口頭契約 ②a verbal promise 口頭承諾

☆ ⁴oral (adj.) 口頭的 ³contract (n.) 合約

【相關字彙】

⁴verb [vɝb] (n.) 動詞

64. ³threat [θrɛt] (n.) ①恐嚇；脅迫；威脅 ②構成威脅的人 (或事物) ③預兆；徵兆

【相關字彙】

³threaten［ˋθrɛtn̩］（v.）①恐嚇；脅迫 ②預示 ③是……的徵兆

65. valiantly［ˋvæljəntlɪ］（adv.）勇敢地

【相關字彙】

⁶valiant［ˋvæljənt］（adj.）勇敢的

66. ³strategy［ˋstrætədʒɪ］（n.）①戰略 ②策略；對策

【相關字彙】

⁶strategic［strəˋtidʒɪk］（adj.）戰略的

67. ¹deal ¹with（phr.）處理

68. ¹run ¹away（phr.）逃跑

69. ³echo ¹with（phr.）發出回聲；回響

【相關字彙】

³echo［ˋɛko］（n.）回音；回聲 （v.）發回聲

70. trembling［ˋtrɛmbl̩ɪŋ］（adj.）顫抖的；發抖的

【相關字彙與重要片語】

³tremble［ˋtrɛmbl̩］（v.）/（n.）發抖；顫抖 （phr.）①tremble at the thought of 一想到……就發抖 ②all of a tremble （口）渾身發抖

～ 第十章 ～
簡訊

據說在八年前，在中國大陸上海（Shanghai），有一位美麗、多才多藝的（⁶versatile）女孩叫做珊珊。她最大的特徵（⁶trait），就是她的眼睛，總像是在天空之中閃耀（⁴twinkle）的星星。珊珊十八歲，她也是一位在校園中非常受歡迎的（²popular）大學生（⁵undergraduate）。有一天，某一件不好的事情發生在她身上。當她搭乘一輛公車到學校，有一件重大的意外事故發生了。雖然她沒有受傷（injured）；卻是，受到非常大的驚嚇。在那之後，她一直做著關於在那一天公車碰撞（³crash）的惡夢。

珊珊所能夠做的就是向學校請求能休息幾天，並且回到她祖母在鄉間的家，因為，她是一位孤兒（³orphan）。她四歲

∽ Chapter 10 ∾
The Text Messages

People say that about eight years ago in [1]Shanghai, [2]Mainland China, there was a beautiful and [3]versatile girl, named Shan-shan, whose utmost [4]trait was that her eyes [5]twinkled like stars in the sky. Shan-shan was eighteen; she was also a very [6]popular [7]undergraduate [8]on campus. One day, something bad [9]happened to her. When she [10]took a bus to school, a terrible accident occurred. Although she was not [11]injured, she got terribly frightened. After that, she kept having nightmares about the bus [12]crash that day.

[13]All Shan-shan could do was request a few days off from the school and go back to her grandmother's house in the

時，雙親就都過世了。祖母養育（¹raise）她很多年了。那時的她需要適當的（³proper）修養一陣子，以便能完全地從創傷（⁶trauma）中恢復正常。

　　另一天，當正覺得十分無聊時，她拿出了她的手機（⁵cellphone）。手機是，意外發生之前，在公車上某處（²somewhere）找到的；但本來的（³original）手機號碼，現在已經被改成是她的了。突然，從這支幾乎還算是嶄新的（²brand-¹new）手機，她接到一封陌生的簡訊。它是一封她以前從來沒看到過的奇怪的簡訊，而她看了一看簡訊。字面上（literally）看來，這是封關於約會的簡訊，而“他”想要她成為他的女朋友。簡訊主要描述（²describe）著：來自於有一名對她來說依然是陌生的男子，對她的許多的讚美（⁴admiration）與欣賞（⁴appreciation）。女孩，出自於她的好奇心，便試著回覆這個發送出這封匿名的（⁶anonymous）簡訊給她的男子，她甚

countryside because she was an ¹⁴orphan. Her parents had both died when she was four. Her grandmother ¹⁵raised her for many years. At that time, she needed to ¹⁶take a ¹⁷proper rest for a while so that she could totally recover from her ¹⁸trauma.

On another day, when she was feeling very bored, she took out her ¹⁹cellphone. It had been found ²⁰somewhere on the bus before the accident happened, but the ²¹original number had already been changed to hers now. ²²All of a sudden, she received a strange ²³text message on this almost still ²⁴brand-new cellphone. It was a strange text message she had never seen before, and she ²⁵took a look at it. The text message was ²⁶literally about dating, and "he" wanted her to be his girlfriend. The text message mainly ²⁷described: a lot of ²⁸admiration and ²⁹appreciation toward her from a man who was still a stranger to her. The girl, out of her curiosity, tried to ³⁰respond to the

至撥打（²dial）了男子的電話號碼。可是，無人接聽電話。那時，她感到有一些兒緊張（⁴tense）有關收到了另一封簡訊。

　　不知爲何這一次，這名男子傳遞了一張他的照片（²photograph）給她。「這名男子是長得很好看的（¹good-looking）」，當珊珊注視著照片，她思索著。另外，她看著這張照片愈久，她愈是對這名男子感覺熟悉。不久，第三封簡訊從這名男子那兒被傳送過來。這封簡訊比起先前的都還更長，而簡訊上頭說道：「妳還記得（¹remember）我嗎？妳在祖母家一切都好嗎？那對我來說是一種極大的（⁴tremendous）痛苦（⁵torture），因爲我再也無法正常地看見妳和妳迷人的雙眼了。我也無法回到我寧靜的（⁶tranquil）生活。自從那場意外發生之後，每件事情都轉變得很多。妳仍然還記得大約是三個星期前，一輛大型公車可怕的（⁵dreadful）意外，造成了一些

man who had sent this [31]anonymous text message to her, and she even [32]dialed the man's phone number. However, nobody [33]answered the phone. At that point, she felt a little [34]tense about receiving another text message.

Without knowing why, the man sent one of his [35]photographs to her this time. "This man is [36]good-looking," thought Shan–shan when she looked at the picture. Moreover, the longer she looked at the photo, the more familiar she felt with the man. Before long, a third text message was sent from the man. The message was longer than before, and it said: "Do you still [37]remember me? Is everything fine at your grandmother's home? It is [38]tremendous [39]torture to me because I cannot see you and your charming eyes in a normal way anymore. I cannot go back to my [40]tranquil life, either. Everything has changed a lot since the accident. Do you still remember the [41]dreadful

人死亡嗎？而我是誰？我就是在死前，在公車上試著跟妳眉來眼去，和對著妳吹口哨的那個人啊！那時，我還對妳眨了眨眼睛，而且，當我想對妳表達（²express）自己的時候，還覺得有點羞怯（bashful）呢！妳能相信嗎？我第一眼見到妳時，我瘋狂地愛上了妳。妳能感受到，當我們在公車上交談時，我的眼睛裡對妳所散發出愛的火花嗎？最後，我也建議（³advise）妳閱讀一本有價值的（³valuable）書，書給取名（⁵entitle）爲《天堂（³heaven）與地獄》。順便一提的是，我想暫時只能經由簡訊與妳溝通了。我就是妳的手機先前的擁有者（²owner）啊！我不知道何時在公車上掉落（²drop）了手機。但那也是爲什麼我能一直知道妳身在何處，和能傳簡訊給妳。」

珊珊大吃一驚（⁵stun），而被這一封簡訊嚇壞了，當這位獨特（⁴unique）男子栩栩如生的（³vivid）的意象，從她公車碰

accident which caused some people to die on the large bus about three weeks ago? And who am I? I am the guy who tried to [42]flirt with you and [43]whistle at you on the bus before I died! I also [44]winked at you and felt a bit [45]bashful while [46]expressing myself to you then. Can you believe it? I [47]fell madly in love with you [48]at first sight. Could you feel that my eyes [49]sparkled with love toward you when we [50]had a talk on the bus? Finally, I also [51]advised you to read a [52]valuable book [53]entitled [54]*Heaven and Hell*. [55]By the way, I think I can only [56]communicate with you through the text messages [57]for now. I am just the previous [58]owner of your cell phone. I [59]have no idea when I [60]dropped it on the bus. But that is also why I can always know where you are and send text messages to you."

Shan-shan was [61]stunned and terrified by this text message as a [62]vivid image of this [63]unique man [64]emerged from her

撞的那一天的記憶（^{2}memory）中浮現出來。就在她昏過去，並在緊急之中被送往醫院接受些許醫療處理之前，她同時地（simultaneously）回想起（^{4}recall）在那時，一名身穿白衣的男人模糊的（^{6}obscure）影像。公車碰撞期間，他被撞到並飛出去公車上的窗戶外面。他接著掉落至地面上，而被另一輛剛好路上經過的轎車（sedan）輾過去。他即刻於混亂之中慘死在車輪之下（^{5}underneath）。

[65]memories in the bus crash that day. Just before she fainted and was sent to a hospital in an emergency to receive some [66]medical care, she [67]simultaneously [68]recalled an [69]obscure image of a man in white at that time. During the bus crash, he was hit and flew outside a window on the bus. He then fell on the ground and was [70]run over by another [71]sedan just [72]passing by on the road. He died [73]underneath the wheels in the chaos immediately.

Chapter 10

Vocabulary

1. Shanghai [ˈʃænˈhaɪ] 上海（大陸城市名）

2. [5]Mainland China 中國大陸

   【相關字彙】

   [5]mainland [ˈmenlənd]（n.）大陸

3. [6]versatile [ˈvɜsətḷ]（adj.）①多才多藝的 ②（感情、氣質等）易變的 （phr.）versatile moods 反覆無常的情緒

4. [6]trait [tret]（n.）特徵；特點；特性

5. [4]twinkle [ˈtwɪŋkḷ]（v.）／（n.）①閃爍；閃光 ②眨眼

6. [2]popular [ˈpɑpjələ]（adj.）①受歡迎的 ②大眾化的；通俗的；民間的 （phr.）①be popular with 受……的歡迎 ②popular superstitions 民間迷信 ③popular fallacies 一般人謬見

   ☆ [5]superstition（n.）迷信　fallacy（n.）謬見；謬誤

   【相關字彙與重要片語】

   [4]popularity [ˌpɑpjəˈlærətɪ]（n.）①名氣；聲望 ②討人喜歡 （phr.）①win popularity 贏得人心；流行 ②enjoy popularity 受歡迎

7. [5]undergraduate [ˌʌndəˈgrædʒuɪt]（n.）大學生

   【相關字彙與重要片語】

   [3]graduate [ˈgrædʒuɪt]（n.）畢業生

　　　　＊［`grædʒʊˏet］（v.）畢業　（phr.）graduate from
　　　　從……畢業

　　　　⁴graduation［ˏgrædʒʊˋeʃən］（n.）畢業　（phr.）a graduation
　　　　ceremony 畢業典禮　☆ ⁵ceremony（n.）儀式；典禮

8. ¹on ³campus（phr.）校園中

　　【相關字彙】

　　³campus［ˋkæmpəs］（n.）校園

9. ¹happen ¹to（phr.）發生於

10. ¹take ¹a ¹bus（phr.）搭公車

11. injured［ɪndʒəd］（adj.）受傷的

　　【相關字彙與重要片語】

　　³injure［ˋɪndʒɚ］（v.）傷害；使負傷；使痛　（phr.）①the
　　injured 負傷者 ②injure one's self-esteem 傷害人的自尊心
　　☆ ⁵esteem（n.）尊重；尊敬

　　³injury［ˋɪndʒərɪ］（n.）負傷；傷害；損害　（phr.）be an
　　injury to 傷害；對……有害

12. ³crash［kræʃ］（v.）/（n.）①碰撞 ②失敗；垮臺；破產 ③
　　（電腦）當機　（phr.）crash into 撞在……上

13. ¹all ¹one ¹can ¹do ¹is V.（phr.）一個人所能做的就是

14. ³orphan［ˋɔrfən］（n.）/（adj.）孤兒（的）　（phr.）an
　　orphan asylum 孤兒院

　　【相關字彙】

　　⁵orphanage［ˋɔrfənɪdʒ］（n.）孤兒院

15. ¹raise [rez] (v.) ①舉起；提高；增加 ②養育 ③籌募；募集 (phr.) ①raise Sb. from the dead 使某人起死回生 ②raise one's voice against 高聲反對（或抗議）

16. ¹take ¹a ¹rest (phr.) 休息

17. ³proper [ˋprɑpɚ] (adj.) ①適當的；適合的 ②正派的；規矩的 ③固有的；特有的 (phr.) ①as you think proper 你認為怎麼合適就 ②proper for the occasion 合時宜
【相關字彙與重要片語】
³property [ˋprɑpətɪ] (n.) ①財產；資產 ②所有物；房地產 ③特性；特質 (phr.) real property 不動產

18. ⁶trauma [ˋtrɔmə] (n.) 創傷

19. ⁵cellphone [ˋsɛlfon] (n.) 手機

20. ²somewhere [ˋsʌmˌhwɛr] (adv.) 在某處

21. ³original [əˋrɪdʒən!] (adj.) ①最初的；本來的 ②獨創的；新穎的 (n.) 原物；原文；原作 (phr.) ①original with ……的獨創 ②true to the original 忠於原文的
【相關字彙與重要片語】
³origin [ˋɔrədʒɪn] (n.) ①起源；發端 ②出身；血統 (phr.) of noble/humble origin 出身高貴/卑賤 的
☆ ²humble (adj.) 謙遜的；卑微的

22. ¹all ¹of ¹a ²sudden (phr.) 突然

23. ³text ²message (phr.) 簡訊
【相關字彙與重要片語】

²message [ˋmɛsɪdʒ]（n.）訊息 （phr.）①wireless message 無線電報 ②leave a message with 給……留個口信

³text [tɛkst]（n.）本文；原文

24. ²brand-¹new [ˋbrændˋnu]（adj.） 嶄新的

【相關字彙與重要片語】

²brand [brænd]（n.）①商標；牌子 ②烙印 ③污名 （v.）①打烙印 ②使蒙受污名 ③加商標於 （phr.）①name brand 品牌；名牌 ②one's own brand of humor 某人別具一格的幽默

25. ¹take ¹a ¹look ¹at（phr.）看一看

26. literally [ˋlɪtərəlɪ]（adv.）字面上地

【相關字彙與重要片語】

⁶literal [ˋlɪtərəl]（adj.）①照字面的；原義的 ②逐字的 （phr.）the literal truth 不折不扣的事實

27. ²describe [dɪˋskraɪb]（v.）①描寫；敘述 ②形容

【相關字彙與重要片語】

³description [dɪˋskrɪpʃən]（n.）①敘述；描寫 ②（物品）說明書 （phr.）be beyond description 非筆墨所能形容

28. ⁴admiration [ˌædməˋreʃən]（n.）讚嘆；讚美

【相關字彙】

³admire [ədˋmaɪr]（v.）讚美；佩服

⁴admirable [ˋædmərəbḷ]（adj.）值得讚賞的

29. ⁴appreciation [əˌpriʃɪˋeʃən]（n.）①鑑賞 ②感謝 ③欣賞

【相關字彙】

³appreciate [ə`priʃɪˌet]（v.）①體會 ②感激 ③欣賞

30. ³respond ¹to（phr.）回答；回應

【相關字彙】

³respond [rɪ`spɑnd]（v.）①回答 ②回應

³response [rɪ`spɑns]（n.）①回答 ②回應

31. ⁶anonymous [ə`nɑnəməs]（adj.）①<u>匿名的</u> ②無特色的；無個性特徵的

32. ²dial [`daɪəl]（v.）撥（電話號碼）

33. ¹answer ¹the ²phone（phr.）接聽電話

34. ⁴tense [tɛns]（adj.）<u>拉緊的；緊張的</u>（n.）時態

35. ²photograph [`fotəˌgræf]（n.）<u>照片</u>（v.）照相

【相關字彙】

²photographer [fə`tɑgrəfɚ]（n.）攝影師

⁴photography [fə`tɑgrəfɪ]（n.）攝影術

⁶photographic [ˌfotə`græfɪk]（adj.）攝影的

36. ¹good-looking [`gʊd`lʊkɪŋ]（adj.）好看的

37. ¹remember [rɪ`mɛmbɚ]（v.）①<u>記得</u> ②記住 ③代……致意；問好（phr.）remember me to Sb. 代我問候某人

38. ⁴tremendous [trɪ`mɛndəs]（adj.）極大的

39. ⁵torture [`tɔrtʃɚ]（v.）/（n.）①<u>痛苦；折磨</u> ②拷問；拷打（phr.）①put Sb. to（the）torture 拷問某人 ②be tortured by unemployment 因失業而苦惱

☆ unemployment（n.）失業

40. ⁶tranquil [ˈtræŋkwɪl]（adj.）寧靜的
【相關字彙】
⁶tranquilizer [ˈtræŋkwɪˌlaɪzɚ]（n.）鎮定劑

41. ⁵dreadful [ˈdrɛdfəl]（adj.）①<u>可怕的</u> ②極其討厭的 （phr.）
a dreadful bore 極其討厭的人
☆ ³bore（n.）令人討厭的人
【相關字彙】
⁴dread [drɛd]（v.）/（n.）恐懼

42. flirt ¹with（phr.）與……調情
【相關字彙】
flirt [flɜt]（v.）調情

43. ³whistle ¹at（phr.）對……吹口哨
【相關字彙】
³whistle [ˈhwɪsl]（v.）/（n.）（吹）口哨

44. ³wink ¹at（phr.） 對……眨眼
【相關字彙與重要片語】
³wink [wɪŋk]（v.）①眨眼 ②（燈光、星星等）閃爍
（n.）①眨眼 ②瞬間 ③閃爍 （phr.）①in a wink 一瞬間
②tip Sb. the/a wink 向某人報信
☆ ²tip（v.）洩漏；告誡

45. bashful [ˈbæʃfəl]（adj.）羞怯的；內向的

46. ²express [ɪkˈsprɛs]（v.）①<u>表示；表達</u> ②快遞 ③搾；擠壓出

（adj.）①快的；直達的　②明確的　（n.）①快車　②快遞

【相關字彙與重要片語】

³expression [ɪkˋsprɛʃən]（n.）①表現法；措辭　②（面容、聲音等的）表情　（phr.）a heart expression of welcome 衷心表示歡迎

³expressive [ɪkˋsprɛsɪv]（adj.）①表現的；有表現力的　②表情豐富的

47. ¹fall madly ¹in ¹love ¹with（phr.）瘋狂愛上某人

48. ¹at ¹first ¹sight（phr.）初見

49. ⁴sparkle ¹with（phr.）因……而發亮

【相關字彙與重要片語】

⁴sparkle [ˋspɑrkl̩]（v.）/（n.）火花；閃爍；閃耀　（phr.）sparkle with wit 妙趣橫生

⁴spark [spɑrk]（n.）火花；火星；閃光　（v.）閃爍

50. ¹have ¹a ¹talk（phr.）談話

51. ³advise [ədˋvaɪz]（v.）①勸告；忠告　②當顧問　③建議

【相關字彙與重要片語】

³advice [ədˋvaɪs]（n.）忠告；建議　（phr.）act on Sb.'s advice 按某人的勸告行事

【諺】Advice when most needed is least heeded. 忠言逆耳。
　　　⁵heed（v）注意

³adviser/³advisor [ədˋvaɪzɚ]（n.）忠告者；建議者；顧問

52. ³valuable [ˋvæljʊəbl̩]（adj.）①貴重的；值錢的　②有價值的

【相關字彙與重要片語】

²value [ˈvælju] (n.) ①價值；價格 ②重要性 (v.) ①估價；評價 ②重視；珍視 (phr.) ①put a high value on 對……評價很高 ②value oneself on 以……自誇

53. ⁵entitle [ɪnˈtaɪtl] (v.) ①給（書籍等）題名；給……取名 ②給予權利（或資格）

54. ³heaven [ˈhɛvən] (n.) ①天空 ②（常大寫）天國；天堂 ③上帝 (phr.) ①Thank Heaven！謝天謝地！幸虧！ ②move heaven and earth 竭盡全力

【諺】Heaven's vengeance is slow but sure.

天網恢恢，疏而不漏。 vengeance (n.) 報復

55. ¹by ¹the ¹way (phr.) 順便一提

56. ³communicate ¹with (phr.) 與……溝通

57. ¹for ¹now (phr.) 暫時；目前

58. ²owner [ˈonɚ] (n.) 持有人；擁有者

【相關字彙與重要片語】

¹own [on] (v.) ①擁有 ②承認 (adj.) ①自己的 ②特有的 (phr.) ①of one's own 屬於自己的 ②on one's own 憑自己；獨立地

59. ¹have ¹no ¹idea (phr.) 毫無所知

【相關字彙與重要片語】

¹idea [aɪˈdiə] (n.) 主意；想法 (phr.) ①give up the idea of 放棄……的念頭 ②get ideas into one's head 抱不切實際

的想法

60. ^{2}drop [drɑp]（v.）①滴下　②掉落；下降　③寄；送；寫（信）　（n.）①（一）滴　②掉落；下降　（phr.）①drop by/in 順便拜訪　②a drop in the ocean/bucket 滄海一粟；九牛一毛　③drop St. like a hot potato/coal 扔掉燙手山芋

☆ ^{3}bucket（n.）水桶　^{2}coal（n.）（燃燒中的）煤塊

【諺】Constant dropping wears the stone. 滴水可穿石。

61. ^{5}stun [stʌn]（v.）①把……打昏；使昏迷　②使大吃一驚；使目瞪口呆

62. ^{3}vivid [ˈvɪvɪd]（adj.）①鮮豔的；鮮明的　②栩栩如生的

63. ^{4}unique [juˈnik]（adj.）/（n.）①獨特的（人或事物）②無與倫比的（人或事物）

64. ^{4}emerge ^{1}from（phr.）自……出現

【相關字彙】

^{4}emerge [ɪˈmɝdʒ]（v.）浮現；出現

65. ^{2}memory [ˈmɛmərɪ]（n.）記憶；回憶　（phr.）①bear/have/keep in memory 記得　②in memory of 紀念；追悼；追憶　③slip Sb.'s memory 使某人一時想不起來

☆ ^{2}slip（v.）錯過；被遺忘

【相關字彙】

^{3}memorize [ˈmɛməˌraɪz]（v.）記住

^{4}memorial [məˈmorɪəl]（n.）紀念館；紀念碑；紀念物

^{4}memorable [ˈmɛmərəbl]（adj.）值得懷念的；難忘的；顯著

的

66. ^{3}medical ^{1}care（phr.）醫療處理（或保健）

67. simultaneously [saɪməlˋtenɪəslɪ]（adv.）同時間地
    【相關字彙】
    ^{6}simultaneous [ˌsaɪmlˋtenɪəs]（adj.）同時的

68. ^{4}recall [rɪˋkɔl]（v.）/（n.）①回憶起；回想 ②召回；召喚

69. obscure [əbˋskjʊr]（adj.）模糊的；不清楚的

70. ^{1}run ^{1}over（phr.）輾過

71. sedan [sɪˋdæn]（n.）轎車

72. ^{1}pass ^{1}by（phr.）經過
    【相關字彙與重要片語】
    ^{1}pass [pæs]（n.）①經過 ②通行證 （v.）①經過 ②（考
    試）及格 ③傳遞 （phr.）①pass down 傳下來 ②pass
    through 經歷；通過

73. ^{5}underneath [ˌʌndɚˋniθ]（prep.）/（adv.）在……的下面

Index 索引
(第X章，第X個單字/片語)

barren 貧瘠的；荒蕪的(1,65)

bashful 羞怯的；內向的(10,45)

basically 在根本上(8,41)

be about to 將要(5,27)

be accessible to 可接近的；可進入的(6,35)

be adjacent to 毗連；鄰近(7,69)

be afraid of 恐怕；害怕(3,20)

be allergic to 對……過敏(2,81)

be aware of 知道(1,179)

be close to 靠近(2,23)

be conscious of 意識到(1,97)

be covered with 被……覆蓋(6,73)

be dressed in 穿著(3,51)

be familiar with 熟悉(9,34)

be fed up with 受夠了(4,25)

be filled with 使充滿(2,31)

be fixed to 被固定在(8,33)

be fond of 喜歡(7,9)

be forced to 被迫(1,25)

(be) full of 充滿著(1,73)

be good at 精通(9,15)

be placed in 被安置；被放置(5,15)

be proud of 驕傲(4,10)

be regretful about 後悔(4,76)

be scared stiff 非常害怕(1,87)

be scared to death 嚇死了(3,67)

be seized with 突然感覺到或被侵擾(9,19)

be sent to 被派到(1,9)

be snowed in 被雪困住(1,72)

be sure to do St. 一定要去做某事(8,45)

be surrounded by 被……包圍(3,83)

be swallowed up 被吞沒(9,22)

be swept away 沖走(9,21)

be tempted to 被誘惑做(8,22)

be unable to V. 無法做(4,39)

(be) willing to 有意願的；情願的(3,14)

because of 由於；因爲(1,158)

beer 啤酒(2,45)

before long 不久(9,16)

behavior 行爲；舉止(1,181)

bench 長凳；長椅(2,70)

Bermingham 伯明罕市(4,2)

beside 在……旁邊(2,35)

beverage 飲料(7,22)

bizarre 奇異的；異乎尋常的(1,180)

blackout 停電(1,18)

bleak 荒涼的(7,55)

blizzard 暴風雪(1,49)

blonde bombshell 金髮碧眼的美女(4,9)

blood-stained 血玷污的(2,108)

bloody 血淋淋；流血的(7,73)

bloom 開花(期)(7,16)

blouse (女用)短上衣；短襯衫(4,70)

blurred 模糊的；難辨別的(2,104)

blush 臉紅(2,65)

boast 自誇；自大(4,11)

Boeing 波音客機(6,3)

boot 長(筒)靴(4,71)

bored 感到無聊的(3,8)

boring 令人生厭的；無聊的(3,11)

box office 售票處(8,47)

brand-new 嶄新的(10,24)

break into 闖入(5,48)

breathe 呼吸(2,90)

bring up 提出(5,94)

broadcast 廣播(6,1)

brochure 小冊子(8,28)

broil 烤；炙(6,71)

brook 小溪；小河(9,24)

broth (用肉、蔬菜等煮成的)清湯(5,37)

brotherhood 兄弟的關係；手足情誼(9,59)

brusquely 粗魯地；粗率地(4,74)

brutally 殘忍地(8,64)

building 建築物(9,41)

burglar 竊賊；強盜(5,47)

burnt 燒焦的(6,70)

burst into 突然發出(8,70)

bury 埋葬(1,88)

bush 灌木(叢)(9,47)

by oneself 獨自(4,44)

by the way 順便一提(10,55)

C

California 加州(8,50)

call for help 求救(2,84)

call 稱呼；取名(2,29)

calm 平靜；冷靜(4,88)

camcorder 手提錄音攝影機(2,99)

campfire 營火(2,60)

camping ground 野營營地(2,50)

Canada 加拿大(1,3)

cancer 癌症(5,6)

candidate 候選人(6,62)

could not but V. 不得不(4,15)

captain 隊長；船長；機長(6,91)

careful 謹慎的；小心的(2,115)

carelessly 不小心地；輕率地；草率地(3,44)

caress 愛撫(4,84)

carry on with 繼續(7,38)

casually 無意地(5,117)

catch on 流行(7,3)

cause 原因(1,162)

cautious 極小心的；慎重的；謹慎的(7,45)

cease 停止；終止(4,79)

cell 細胞(5,9)

cellphone 手機(10,19)

cemetery 墓地；公墓(7,27)

centimeter 公分(4,8)

changeable 易變的；善變的(1,20)

chaos 混亂狀態；混沌(6,56)

charming 迷人的(4,6)

chase 追趕(3,75)

chatter 喋喋不休地說(7,41)

check out 檢查(7,47)

chemistry 激情；來電(4,5)

cherry blossom 櫻花(7,15)

chicken 膽怯的(9,57)

childhood 童年時期(7,4)

childlike 孩子般的(7,79)

choose 選擇(8,49)

chop 切碎；剁細(6,77)

chubby 圓胖的；豐滿的(1,89)

chuckle 咯咯笑(4,89)

cinema 戲院；電影院(8,23)

circular 圓形的(7,43)

cleanse 使清潔；清理(8,72)

cling to 緊握不放；緊抓(7,70)

clinic 診所(5,11)

closely 接近地；細心地(1,60)

clumsily 笨拙地(4,80)

clutch 緊緊抓牢(9,18)

come back 回來(1,105)

come from 來自(5,52)

come out 出現(2,109)

come to an end 結束(1,96)

come to 來到(1,64)

come to 突然想起(4,18)

comfort 安慰(4,81)

commemorate 慶祝；紀念(2,75)

commercial 商業的(8,29)

commit suicide 自殺(1,149)

communicate with 與……溝通(10,56)

communication 溝通；交流(4,33)

company 陪伴(4,53)

competition 競爭；比賽(7,39)

complain 抱怨(1,61)

complete 完全的(3,50)

complexion 臉色；面容(5,77)

condemn 譴責；責備(4,90)

condition 條件(5,89)

confirm 證實(2,119)

consecutive 連續的(8,55)

consent 同意；答應(5,98)

consequently 因此；所以(6,39)

consider 視為；認為(1,157)

constantly 接連不斷地(5,45)

continue 繼續(7,34)

continuous 繼續的；連續的(1,111)

control 控制；支配；抑制(4,16)

corner 角；街角(5,57)

corpse 屍體(6,59)

costume 服裝；裝束(4,60)

cottage 小屋(1,93)

disease 疾病(5,83)

disgusting 噁心的(6,76)

disrespectfully 不尊重地(3,45)

distant 遙遠的(1,66)

distorted 扭曲的(7,75)

do not have a clue about 關於……一無所知；毫無頭緒(5,50)

do one's best 全力以赴(1,107)

do something different 做不一樣的事(3,9)

downstream 下游的(地)(9,43)

dramatically 戲劇地(6,51)

drape 窗簾；帷幔(5,25)

drastically 激烈地；猛烈地(5,69)

dreadful 可怕的(10,41)

drop 掉落(10,60)

drug 藥(5,67)

due to 由於(1,40)

E

each time 每次(1,108)

echo with 發出回聲；回響(9,69)

efficiently 有效率地(6,47)

elder 年紀較長的(2,14)

electric/electrical 電的(1,24)

electrocardiogram 心電圖(5,109)

emerge from 自……出現(10,64)

emergency 緊急事件(2,88)

endlessly 無止盡地(1,168)

endure 忍耐；忍受(4,28)

England 英國；英格蘭(4,3)

enigmatic 如謎的；難理解的(6,17)

enjoy 享受；喜愛(2,39)

enough 足夠的(2,87)

ensue 隨後發生；接踵而來(6,49)

entertaining 使人愉悅的；有趣的(2,62)

enthusiastic 狂熱的；熱心的(3,89)

entitle 給(書籍等)題名；給……取名(10,53)

entrance 進入；入學；入場(6,94)

eruption 爆發；噴出(6,74)

escape from 躲避(1,33)

establish 建立；創立(6,18)

eventually 最終地(6,30)

exact 確切的(5,107)

except for 除了……以外(4,24)

exchange 交換(2,61)

excitement 興奮；刺激(3,10)

exhaust from 使筋疲力竭(9,36)

existence 存在(3,99)

exotic 異國情調的(7,31)

expectation 期待；預期(3,73)

experience 經驗；遭受(1,170)

expert 專家(1,155)

explain 說明；解釋(3,93)

explanation 說明；解釋(6,90)

explore 探險；探索(9,13)

express 表示；表達(10,46)

extra 額外的(地)；特別的(地)(7,44)

eyeball 眼球(3,74)

F

face 面臨；面向(3,37)

fail to 失敗；未能(7,60)

faint 微弱的；模糊的(3,78)

fall asleep 睡著(5,38)

fall down 倒下(2,92)

fall into a deep sleep 沉睡(5,106)

fall madly in love with 瘋狂愛上某人(10,47)

famous 有名的；著名的(1,5)

farther 更遠；進一步(7,65)

fasten 繫緊(6,100)

fearful 可怕的(1,98)

feather 羽毛(7,32)

feel like 想要；感到好似(1,68)

feel sleepy 想睡(5,65)

female 女性(的)；雌性(的)(3,72)

fiercely 猛烈地；狂暴地(6,109)

fight 爭吵(4,38)

film 影片；電影(8,34)

finally 最終地；最後地(1,148)

finished 完蛋了的(1,142)

firefighter 消防員(6,41)

firmly 堅固地；牢牢地(2,111)

first aid 急救(5,14)

fix 修理(1,16)

flee 逃離；逃走(3,88)

flight recorder 飛機黑盒子(6,86)

flight 飛機(6,4)

flirt with 與……調情(10,42)

float 漂浮(3,61)

Florida 佛羅里達州(6,15)

fly to 飛往(6,5)

fog 霧；濃霧；煙霧(6,97)

footstep 腳步(聲)(9,48)

for a very long time 很久的時間(6,38)

for a while 暫時；一會兒(3,49)

for example 例如(1,103)

for life 一生(7,13)

for now 暫時；目前(10,57)

for seconds 幾秒鐘(1,134)

for the last time 最後一次(5,34)

forget about 忘記(9,58)

forgive 原諒；寬恕(1,147)

formal 正式的(5,28)

fortieth 第四十(的)(5,119)

fragile 脆弱的(5,64)

freezing 冰冷的；嚴寒的(5,71)

frequent 時常發生的；屢次的(1,110)

fried 油炸的 (2,46)

frighten 使害怕；使驚恐 (2,103)

frightful 恐怖的 (3,95)

frontier 國境；邊境 (1,14)

frozen 冰凍的 (6,72)

function 起作用 (5,68)

furthermore 而且；此外；再者 (1,160)

G

game 遊戲 (7,2)

gas 油門 (3,69)

gate 大門(口) (8,25)

gentleman 紳士 (5,33)

gently 輕輕地；柔和地 (4,85)

get a clear picture of 清楚了解 (1,55)

get a ride from 讓某人搭車 (3,53)

get away from 逃離 (3,71)

get on with 繼續做 (7,57)

get rid of 擺脫 (1,109)

get up 起床 (1,78)

ghost 幽靈；鬼 (1,113)

ghostly 幽靈(似)的 (9,54)

go back to 返回 (6,87)

go by 時間流逝 (6,104)

go caming 露營 (2,25)

go crazy 發瘋 (4,49)

go for a ride (騎/開車)兜風；騎馬出遊

(8,6)

go from bad to worse 愈來愈糟糕 (1,101)

go to bed 上床睡覺 (1,143)

go too far 做事情太過分 (4,77)

gone 不見的 (6,19)

good-looking 好看的 (10,36)

gorgeous 非常漂亮的；像大美人的 (8,63)

gorilla 大猩猩 (4,58)

gossip 說閒話；流言蜚語 (6,105)

government 政府 (1,10)

grab 抓取；搶奪 (1,90)

gradually 逐漸地 (4,86)

grave 墓穴 (3,41)

greedily 貪婪地 (2,38)

grief 悲傷；悲痛 (9,50)

grim 陰森的；猙獰的 (4,96)

grow 增加 (1,100)

guess 推測；猜想 (1,57)

gunshot 射擊 (1,153)

gusts of (一)陣陣 (5,70)

gut(s) 膽量(複數) (6,65)

guy 傢伙；人 (4,55)

H

habit 習慣；習性 (4,26)

hang 懸；掛(3,96)

happen to 發生於(10,9)

happen 發生(1,128)

hard 努力地；拼命地(1,52)

harm 傷害；損害(5,90)

harsh 刺耳的(6,111)

hasten 趕緊；催促(2,83)

hatred 憎恨(8,83)

haunt 糾纏(某人)(9,53)

have a talk 談話(10,50)

have been to 曾經去過(6,115)

have no idea 毫無所知(10,59)

have nothing in particular to do 沒什麼
特別要做的事(8,3)

have something in common with 與……
有共同點(3,19)

headgear 頭套；頭飾(4,61)

health 健康(5,21)

heartbeat 心跳(5,108)

heaven 天國；天堂(10,54)

heavily 猛烈地(1,22)

hell 地獄(6,116)

hesitate 躊躇；猶豫(5,91)

hide 遮蔽；躲藏(1,26)

hideous 極醜陋的(7,74)

history 歷史(2,118)

hit 襲擊(5,72)

hoarse 嘶啞的(5,79)

hometown 故鄉；家鄉(1,63)

horrible 恐怖的；可怕的(2,20)

horrify 使恐懼；使驚懼(5,115)

horrifying 令人恐懼的；不寒而慄的
(8,58)

hot spring 溫泉(9,8)

however 然而；可是(3,59)

howl (狼)嗥叫(7,54)

Hualien County 花蓮縣(9,5)

huge 巨大的(8,14)

hundred 百(的)(4,7)

hurt 使傷害(4,57)

hustle and bustle 喧鬧聲(6,108)

hysterical 歇斯底里的(1,135)

I

identification/ID 身分證(6,60)

identify 辨識；認出(7,66)

illness 疾病(1,159)

illusion 幻覺；錯覺(1,169)

image 影像(2,105)

imagine 想像(6,55)

immediately 立即地；馬上地(2,91)

important 重要的(5,93)

improper 不適當的(3,34)

in a hurry 匆忙地(3,85)

in a state of 在……的狀況(6,110)

in a(n)… way 以……的方式(6,16)

in accordance with 與……一致；依照(3,55)

in addition 另外(5,95)

in advance 事先(2,22)

in agony 在極度痛苦中(5,7)

in an instant 不久(5,105)

in exchange for 交換(5,87)

in fact 事實上(7,48)

in front of 在……的前面(1,121)

in one's youth 某人年輕時期(2,68)

in other words 換句話說(6,80)

in the end 最終(6,107)

in the meantime 在……期間；同時(8,44)

in the middle of nowhere 鳥不生蛋(1,69)

in the past 在過去(1,32)

in the very beginning 最開始(2,12)

in total 總共(3,6)

incident 事件(2,95)

incomprehensible 無法理解的(1,127)

increasingly 增加地(4,51)

incurable 不能醫治的；無可救藥的(5,82)

indoors 在屋內；在室內(9,61)

ineffective 無效的(4,32)

inevitably 必然地；不可避免地(9,28)

inform Sb. of St. 通知某人事情(5,114)

inhabitant 居民(1,31)

inhumane 無人性的；殘忍的(6,82)

injured 受傷的(10,11)

instead of 代替；而不是(8,76)

intend to 打算(9,52)

intensive care unit 加護病房(5,16)

intentionally 企圖地；故意地(5,73)

interesting 有趣的(7,1)

intersection 十字路口(4,64)

into thin air 無影無蹤(5,113)

investigation 調查；研究(2,116)

iron 鐵(2,34)

issue 發出(6,22)

it is a pity that 很可惜的是；真遺憾(9,25)

it is said that 據說(3,1)

it is time for 該是……時候了(7,50)

J

joke 玩笑；笑話(3,31)

joy 歡樂；高興(8,7)

jump 跳躍(4,72)

K

keep an eye on 特別注意(7,63)

masculine 男性的；男子氣概的(3,4)

mask 面具(4,93)

massacre 大屠殺；殘殺(6,83)

mayoral 市長的(6,68)

meal 一餐(2,58)

meat 肉類(6,78)

medical care 醫療處理
（或保健）(10,66)

medical 醫學的；醫療的(2,100)

mellow （酒）芳醇的(2,44)

memory 記憶；回憶(10,65)

mentally 內心地(1,86)

mention 提及；說到；寫到(1,166)

Michigan 密西根州(2,9)

might 或許(5,31)

miraculously 奇蹟地(5,112)

mission 任務；使命(1,8)

mixed 多種不同的(8,36)

monster 怪物；怪獸(7,68)

mood 情緒；心情(4,87)

morbid 變態的；病態的(8,65)

moreover 此外；並且(3,32)

mortuary 停屍間(6,34)

motionlessly 不動地；靜止地(5,60)

move into 搬入(5,18)

move 搬動；移動(1,178)

movie theater 電影院(8,13)

murder 謀殺(8,59)

murderer 兇手(8,66)

musician 音樂家(5,4)

mysterious 神祕的；不可思議的(2,1)

mystery 謎；神祕；不可思議的事(6,10)

N

name 給……取名；給……命名(5,5)

narrate 敘述；說明(2,10)

nasty 令人厭惡的；令人作嘔的(6,48)

native 本土的；本國的(2,122)

nearby 附近的(2,28)

necessary 必要的；必須的(2,86)

neighboring 鄰近的(1,27)

neither （兩者之中）無一個(9,14)

nervous breakdown 精神崩潰(1,130)

news 新聞；報導；消息(5,36)

next to 在……旁(3,63)

next-door 隔壁的(7,18)

night drive 夜遊(3,26)

nightmare 惡夢(2,11)

nighttime 夜間(5,39)

normal 正常的；標準的；普通的(4,36)

northern 北部的；北方的(1,11)

not… anymore 不再(4,27)

not… at all 一點也不(3,21)

note 便條(4,52)

notice 注意(3,65)

notorious 惡名昭彰的(6,7)

numerous 無數的；很多的(4,31)

O

obscure 模糊的；不清楚的(10,69)

observation 觀察；觀察力(7,46)

obviously 明顯地(5,24)

occasion 機會(7,17)

occupy 使忙碌(2,53)

odd 奇怪的；怪異的(4,17)

of course 當然(5,88)

of the utmost importance 極為重要
(6,85)

on and on 繼續不停地(7,42)

on campus 校園中(10,8)

on foot 步行(8,26)

on holiday 在休假中(8,2)

on a corner of 在……的轉角(8,15)

on the outskirts of 在……郊外(9,4)

on the shore 在岸邊(9,33)

on the way 在途中(3,25)

once again 再一次(1,92)

once in a while 偶爾(4,45)

once upon a time 從前(2,13)

one by one 一個接一個(8,79)

open up 開張；開門營業(8,18)

orginally 起初；原來(4,41)

original 最初的；本來的(10,21)

orphan 孤兒(10,14)

out of 出於(1,174)

overall 整體；全部(8,53)

owing to 由於(9,30)

owner 持有人；擁有者(10,58)

P

paddle 用槳划船(2,36)

page 頁(1,140)

pain 痛苦；疼痛(5,41)

panic 恐慌；驚慌(1,124)

paper, scissors, stone 剪刀；石頭；布
(7,23)

parking lot 停車場(8,24)

partially 部分地(5,74)

particular 特定的；特別的(3,27)

pass by 經過(10,72)

passenger 乘客；旅客(3,62)

path 小路；小徑(3,81)

patient 病人(5,23)

pattern 圖案；圖形(7,28)

pause 中斷；暫停(7,37)

pay attention to 注意(3,90)

pay 付(5,86)

peculiar 獨特的(4,42)

peel off 去掉；脫掉(4,91)

perfect 完美的(4,12)

perform 做;完成(2,85)

periodically 定期地;間歇地(6,23)

personality 人格;個性(3,18)

personnel (總稱)人員(6,29)

Philippines 菲律賓(5,2)

photograph 照片(10,35)

physical 肉體的;身體的(5,40)

pinch 捏;掐;擰;夾(2,112)

plan to 計畫去做(9,2)

play a trick on Sb. 對某人惡作劇(4,21)

playmate 玩伴(7,6)

plenty of 很多的(6,64)

pneumonia 肺炎(1,41)

point at 指著(3,42)

point out 指出(1,164)

polar 北極的;南極的;極地的(1,13)

political 政治的(6,61)

pollen 花粉(2,82)

poor 可憐的;不幸的(1,44)

popular 受歡迎的(10,6)

position 職位(6,69)

possible 可能的(1,172)

poster 海報(8,32)

powerful 強大的(8,19)

pray for 祈禱(4,83)

prepare 準備;預備(2,73)

present 呈現(8,54)

previously 以前地;先前地(4,63)

price 代價(7,10)

primary school 小學(7,7)

print 印;印刷(8,31)

private 私人的(2,7)

probably 大概地;很可能地(1,58)

problem 問題(1,19)

process 過程(1,23)

produce 生產;產生(6,103)

professional 專業的(5,13)

proliferation 增加;擴散(5,8)

promise 答應;允諾(4,62)

proper 適當的;適合的(10,17)

protagonist 主角(4,66)

prove 證明;證實(3,98)

psychologically 心理(學)地(9,32)

psychologist 心理學家(1,173)

pull a prank 惡作劇(4,56)

put on 穿上(4,59)

put up the tent 搭帳篷(2,55)

put up with 忍受(4,50)

Q

quality 特質;特性(4,43)

quarrel 口角;爭吵(4,37)

question 問題(5,118)

R

raise 養育(10,15)

rapid 快的；急促的(9,17)

rare 珍奇的；稀罕的(2,57)

reach an agreement with Sb. 與某人達成協議(5,104)

reach 達到；到達(2,16)

realize 了解；領悟(3,94)

reappearance 再現(1,112)

reason 理由；動機(4,23)

reasonable 合理的(6,89)

recall 回憶起；回想(10,68)

receive 接受(5,12)

record 錄製(2,97)

recover from 從……恢復過來(5,85)

recover 恢復；復原；痊癒(5,20)

recurrent 一再發生的；循環的 (6,11)

red light, green light 一二三木頭人(7,5)

regarding 關於(4,34)

relax 使輕鬆；放輕鬆(8,5)

rely on 依賴(5,61)

remain 仍是；保持(6,36)

remember 記得(10,37)

remove 脫掉(4,92)

report 報告；報導(1,4)

request 請求；請願(6,25)

rescue 援救(1,151)

resist 反抗；抵抗(5,54)

respect 尊敬；尊重(3,39)

respirator 呼吸器(5,62)

respond to 回答；回應(10,30)

result from 因……而產生(5,42)

result in 導致……的結果(7,11)

resurface 再次浮出；再次露出(9,27)

retaliate 報復(4,22)

retrieve 重新得到；收回(6,84)

return 返回(2,114)

reveal 揭露；揭示(6,2)

review 批評；評論(8,37)

revive 使甦醒(2,93)

rifle 來福槍；步槍(1,131)

right away 馬上(1,122)

rigid 僵硬的(1,91)

riverbed 河床(9,42)

round 一回合；一輪(7,60)

route 路線；航線(9,35)

routine 例行公事；日常工作(1,71)

rub Sb. the wrong way 惹惱某人(7,33)

rude 無禮的；粗魯的(3,29)

ruins 廢墟；遺跡(9,40)

run away 逃跑(9,68)

run for 競選(6,67)

run out of 自……跑出(3,84)

run over 輾過(10,70)

runway 機場跑道(6,32)

ruthlessly 冷酷地；無情地(8,56)

S

satisfactory 令人滿意的(8,42)

satisfied 感到滿意的(1,138)

sauce 調味醬；醬汁(6,79)

savage 殘酷的；兇猛的(6,81)

scary 嚇人的；可怕的(1,126)

scatter 散佈；撒播(6,57)

scene 景色；景象(2,102)

school of (魚)群(2,43)

scream 尖叫(聲)(1,118)

seat belt 安全帶(6,101)

sedan 轎車(10,71)

seemingly 表面上；似乎是(8,81)

sentimental 深情的；多愁善感的(2,67)

separate 分開的；個別的(6,58)

serial 連續的(8,51)

serious 嚴重的(1,17)

set in (指雨、壞天氣、傳染等)
開始並可能繼續下去(1,42)

set up camp 搭帳篷(2,54)

seven holes bleed 七孔流血(4,95)

severe 嚴重的(1,36)

shadow 映象(3,97)

shadowy 幽靈般的(7,67)

Shanghai 上海(10,1)

share 共有(9,60)

shiver with fear 嚇得發抖(1,125)

shocked 震驚的(1,83)

shoot 開槍(1,133)

shout 呼喊；喊叫(7,24)

show up 出現(1,167)

show 顯示(3,38)

shriek 尖叫(3,64)

side effect 副作用(5,66)

sight 景象(6,52)

sign 徵兆(3,76)

signal 信號；暗號(6,20)

silently 寂靜地；無聲地(5,59)

simultaneously 同時間地(10,67)

situation 情況(1,95)

skull 骷髏頭；頭骨(8,78)

slaughter 屠殺；屠宰(2,124)

sleepwalk 夢遊(1,176)

slight 輕微的；少許的(3,23)

smoothly 平靜地；安穩地(5,43)

snow 雪；下雪(1,21)

snowstorm 暴風雪(1,35)

so that 如此……以至於(1,54)

somewhat 有點；稍微(7,72)

somewhere 在某處(10,20)

soon after 不久之後(4,67)

soul 靈魂；魂魄(6,54)

sound 聽起來(1,76)

temporary 暫時的；臨時的（4,46）

tenderly 溫柔地（2,66）

tense 拉緊的；緊張的（10,34）

terrible 恐怖的；可怕的（1,34）

terrifying 令人害怕的（8,80）

territory 區域（1,12）

test 測驗；檢驗（6,88）

text message 簡訊（10,23）

thanks to 由於（6,27）

that is 換句話說（5,99）

the Bermuda Triangle 百慕達三角洲（6,8）

thereafter 之後；以後（1,114）

therefore 因此（3,54）

thereupon 隨即；立即（6,92）

threat 恐嚇；脅迫；威脅（9,64）

ticket 票；入場券（8,46）

times 時代；年代（2,121）

title 標題；名稱（8,48）

to be on the safe side 為了保險起見（9,38）

to make matters worse 更糟的是（9,49）

tolerate 忍受；忍耐；寬容（9,62）

tomb 墳墓；墓碑（3,43）

tool 工具（6,46）

torture 痛苦；折磨（10,39）

totem 圖騰（像）（7,29）

tourist 觀光客（9,11）

trace 絲毫；少許（3,79）

trait 特徵；特點；特性（10,4）

tranquil 寧靜的（10,40）

transfer 轉移；調動（5,10）

transparent 透明的（2,26）

trauma 創傷（10,18）

treatment 治療（法）（2,89）

trembling 顫抖的；發抖的（9,70）

tremendous 極大的（10,38）

tribe 種族；部落（2,123）

true 真的；確實的（1,1）

try one's best 盡全力；盡最大努力（3,92）

tulip 鬱金香（7,14）

turn around 轉身（7,62）

turn one's stomach 讓人反感（或噁心）（6,50）

turn 變得；成為（4,29）

tutor 家庭教師（2,5）

twinkle 閃爍；閃光（10,5）

type 類型（4,54）

U

under the weather 不舒服（7,61）

undercurrent 暗流（9,23）

undergo 遭受；遭遇（6,106）

undergraduate 大學生（10,7）

underground 地面下（2,3）

underneath 在……的下面（10,73）

understand 理解;懂(5,76)

unexpectedly 無預期地;出乎意料地 (6,21)

unfamiliar 陌生的;不熟悉的(8,16)

unforeseen 未預見到的;難以預料的 (9,31)

unfortunately 不幸地(1,37)

unintentionally 非故意地(2,96)

unique 獨特的(10,63)

unknown 未知的(1,30)

unload 卸(貨)(2,51)

unlock 開……的鎖(6,44)

unlucky 不吉利的(7,35)

unnamed 未命名的(7,49)

unrecognizable 無法認出的(6,113)

untidy 不整齊的(3,40)

unusual 異常的;奇怪的(6,96)

upon 在……後立即(2,48)

use up 用完(6,42)

V

vacant 空虛的(8,4)

vaguely 不清晰地;模糊地(2,107)

valiantly 勇敢地(9,65)

valley 溪谷;峽谷(9,6)

valuable 有價值的(10,52)

Vancouver 溫哥華(1,56)

vanish 消失;消散(8,77)

vanity 虛榮(8,67)

various 各式各樣的;不同種類的(6,45)

vast 廣大的;廣闊的(8,75)

vehicle 交通工具;車輛(9,3)

verbal 口頭的(9,63)

versatile 多才多藝的(10,3)

village 村落;村莊(3,13)

visit 參觀;遊覽(9,12)

vivid 栩栩如生的(10,62)

voice 聲音(5,80)

vulgar 粗俗的;粗鄙的(3,30)

W

wail 嚎啕大哭;哀泣(8,71)

wait for 等待(4,65)

wake up 醒來(1,116)

walk into 走進(1,79)

ward 病房(5,17)

warmth 體溫(9,29)

warn 警告(7,36)

warning 告誡(3,66)

waterfall 瀑布(2,27)

wave 揮手(3,52)

weak 弱的;虛弱的(5,63)

wear 穿;佩帶(7,76)

weary 疲勞的(8,10)

wedding anniversary 結婚紀念日(5,120)

weird 怪誕的；神祕的；鬼怪似的(1,94)

what's more 而且；此外(6,75)

whatever 不論什麼(5,102)

wheelchair 輪椅(5,110)

whenever 每當(1,104)

whistle at 對……吹口哨(10,43)

wild 荒野(2,59)

wilderness 荒野(3,15)

wildlife 野生生物(9,7)

wink at 對……眨眼(10,44)

winner 勝利者(7,21)

wipe off 擦掉(8,12)

witty 機智的(6,63)

wonder 對……感到疑惑(5,49)

wonderful 美好的(2,76)

wooden 木製的(1,84)

word of mouth 口碑(8,40)

work for 爲……工作(2,6)

worry 令人發愁的事
(或人)(1,144)

worse 更糟(4,30)

worthwhile 值得做的(9,10)

write down 把……寫下(1,139)

yawn (打)呵欠(8,11)

yearn for 嚮往；渴望(9,44)

Y

yard 庭院；院子(2,4)

Notes

Notes

Notes

Notes

語言學習機（4）

鬼書 **1** *The Book of Ghosts Book 1*

建議售價・379元

作　　者：子星
校　　對：子星
插　　畫：藝想工作室
專案主編：徐錦淳
編輯部：徐錦淳、黃麗穎、劉承薇、林榮威
設計部：張禮南、何佳諠、賴澧淳
經銷部：林琬婷、莊博亞
業務部：張輝潭、焦正偉、吳適意
發行人：張輝潭
出版發行：白象文化事業有限公司
　　　　　402台中市南區美村路二段392號
　　　　　出版、購書專線：（04）2265-2939
　　　　　傳真：（04）2265-1171
印　　刷：基盛印刷工場
版　　次：2012年（民101）八月初版一刷

國家圖書館出版品預行編目資料

鬼書1／子星著．—初版．—臺中市：白象文
化，民101.08
　　　面：　公分．——（語言學習機；4）
ISBN 978-986-5979-21-8（平裝）
1.英語　2.讀本
805.18　　　　　　　　　　　101004374

設計編印

印書小舖

網　　址：www.ElephantWhite.com.tw
電　　郵：press.store@msa.hinet.net